Secrets

BEAUTIES FROM ASHES SERIES
BOOK 1

Endorsements

If C.S. Lewis were to rewrite *The Screwtape Letters* focusing on the trials and tribulations of modern high school girls, it would read like Beckie Lindsey's *Beauties from Ashes* series. This powerful story will remind you that you do not battle against yourself or other people, but against the devil. Read it with the lights on. Then, rest peacefully, knowing that God loves you and protects you. —**Ashley Jones**, author

In her first novel, *Secrets*, in the Beauties from Ashes series, Beckie Lindsey proves she is not only a gifted storyteller, but a woman with a great heart for and understanding of the plights which plague so many teens in our modern era. Beckie's inviting prose, along with the perfect weaving together of characters and plot, will keep both teens and adults entranced until the last page is turned. Secrets is a brilliantly written book you'll want to read again and again. Guaranteed!"—**Martha Jane Orlando**, author of *A Trip, a Tryst and a Terror, Children in the Garden, The Moment of Truth, Revenge!, Redemption,* and *Revelation*

Secrets

BEAUTIES FROM ASHES SERIES
BOOK 1

BECKIE LINDSEY

Elk Lake
PUBLISHING, INC.
35 Dogwood Drive
Plymouth, MA 02360

Copyright Notice

Cover Design: Jeff Gifford
Interior Design: Cheryl L. Childers
Editors: Molly Jo Realy, Cristel Phelps, Deb Haggerty
Published in Association with Hartline Literary Agency.
PUBLISHED BY: Elk Lake Publishing, Inc., 35 Dogwood Dr., Plymouth, MA 02360

Names: Lindsey, Beckie (Beckie Lindsey)
Secrets: Book One Beauties from Ashes Series / Beckie Lindsey
266 p. 23cm × 15cm (9 in. × 6 in.)
Description: Every girl has a secret she hopes the light will never find—but the demons already have. Four girls. Four sets of secrets. Four searching for answers.
Identifiers: ISBN-13: 978-1-946638-63-2 (trade) | 978-1-946638-64-9 (POD) | 978-1-946638-65-6 (e-book.)
Key Words: teens, problems, girls, popularity, body image, positive self-image, demons.
LCCN: 2018930402 Fiction

Dedication

To Linda S. Pate
January 23, 2012
"See You Soon."

Acknowledgments

My Lord and Savior, Jesus Christ—I desire to live a life worthy of Your calling. I want everything I write to be out of love for You. "Oh, that my actions would consistently reflect your decrees! Then I will not be ashamed when I compare my life with your commands. As I learn your righteous regulations, I will thank you by living as I should" (Psalm 119:5-7 NLV). "You are good and do only good; teach me your decrees" (Psalm 119:68 NLV).

My amazing husband and best friend—Scott, I love you more than you'll ever know. I'm blessed to be on this journey with you at my side. I'm so excited about this next chapter of our lives together.
My family—Kevin, Chad, Charity, Katie, Michelle, and Daddy, I couldn't ask for a more loving and supportive family. Thanks for always being there, the prayers, and words of encouragement. Special thanks to Charity, Katie, and Noah for your tireless proofreading, edits, and faith in me. I love you all.

My dear friends—Krystal, Sue, Tammi, and Kym, I treasure each of you. Our friendship and the trials the Lord has brought us through helped inspire my writing. Thanks for always pointing me toward Jesus and sticking by me even when I'm not fun to be around. I love you sisters!

My church family—High Desert Church, I am blessed beyond measure to attend and serve with such a selfless kingdom-minded group of pastors. Women on the board of Thursday morning Bible study, I'm honored to call you my sisters and friends. Special thanks to my partner in ministry for over ten years, Wendy Stine, and my sweet friend and co-author of *Legacy*, Patty Schell. Love you, girls.
My critique group—Patty, Rebekah, Karla, and Cassidy, I cannot thank you gals enough for your friendship, honest critiques, humble suggestions, and prayers. I couldn't have done this without each of you.

My amazing editor and friend—Molly Jo Realy, this book wouldn't have happened without you. Thanks for your prayers and belief in me as a writer. You braved the wilderness of run-on sentences, spelling, and grammar issues while somehow managing to keep me encouraged. Thanks for everything.

My agents—Cyle Young and Associate Agent Tessa Hall, you both are amazing. Cyle, thanks for teaching me your Polishing Course. Tessa, thanks for finding my submission in the huge pile then guiding me through the dreaded proposal process.

Elk Lake Publishing Inc.—Deb, you listened to my fifteen-minute pitch that I rattled off in only seven minutes and decided to take a chance on me. Thanks for your kindness, patience, and wisdom. Cristel, thanks for your to-the-point edits, sense of humor and words of encouragement. You guys are great. I'm honored to be a part of the Elk Lake family.

And last but not least, to YOU—Thank you for reading this book! I hope my writing points you to the One who loves you more than ever, Jesus Christ.

Trigger

Warning

READERS, please be advised that *Secrets: Book One Beauties from Ashes Series* includes themes and events surrounding sexual trauma, depression, and suicide. Those of you who are experiencing, or who have experienced these issues, may find some of the content emotionally distressing and/or triggering. Triggering is defined as heightened feelings or memories associated with a traumatic experience when exposed to descriptions or similar events that are reminiscent of the experienced trauma. If this occurs, please stop reading and consult with a licensed mental health professional who specializes in the treatment of sexual trauma, depression, or suicide.

If you have experienced sexual traumas or thought about suicide and have never talked about it with anyone, I encourage you to *tell* a trusted adult. I also encourage you to talk to a licensed mental health professional who can help you walk through the first steps of healing.

Arcana

SILAS felt their arrival before he could see them. The gooseflesh on his forearms indicated they were near. He stood guard on a bluff overlooking the small town of Arcana. A sudden gust of wind blew a golden strand of hair across his rigid jaw.

A storm was brewing.

Lightning streaked through the moonless sky. At least two hundred covert creatures were illuminated as if caught in a strobe light. They jerked and staggered robotically, then vanished back into the night. These creatures were the reason Silas was here and waited for further orders.

Moments later, another streak of lightning cut the night. But this one was different. This streak was headed directly for him. A burst of white light revealed a terrifying being. The massive angel was a head taller than Silas, himself over eight feet tall. The larger angel had the face of a man, but with fierce lion-like features and towering wings covered all over with human eyes. He was dressed for war with a helmet, a golden breastplate and an enormous sword.

"Greetings, Philo. I'm ready."

Philo removed a small scroll from his thick belt, extending his muscular arm. "Everything you need to know is here."

Silas unrolled and read the scroll. He nodded then put it in his mouth and swallowed. No one else would see it.

Philo gave a nod. "The four girls are now in your care." His deep, throaty voice resounded. "We anticipate much opposition from the enemy. Do not hesitate to call for assistance. The Almighty's army is behind you."

Silas bowed. "It is my honor to be in the Lord's service."

———————

At the same time, another meeting was taking place in the recesses of the city's bowels. A serpentine, gravel road led to a neon sign flickering only half its letters in front of a tired building. Tucked away in the basement of the seedy motel, notorious and accursed for five murders throughout its history, the meeting commenced.

A large creature with the torso of a man and the head of a raven stood behind the lectern. "Order! I call this meeting to order!" The thing cackled, flailing its dark, ragged wings.

The cacophony of shrieks and snorts lowered, but the room still hummed like a beehive. Lights in the room flickered, revealing a horned leviathan materializing from a cloud of sulfuric smoke. The monster let loose a howl that sent the man-raven spinning uncontrollably in mid-air while the other creatures craned their necks, watching helplessly until the creature dropped like a limp towel on the floor.

Not another sound was heard until the horned beast, Bellian, spoke.

"We have been summoned here by the high priest himself," The beast growled, exposing its jagged teeth. "Each of us need to consider ourselves on call at all times. Our assignment is these four girls." The beast pointed its gnarled, bony finger to a hologram that showed individual photos of the girls and their current location—Arcana High School of Arts and Technology. "Once we have identified their weaknesses, we will be assigned specific duties."

Each uniquely deformed demon gawked at the hologram, some drooling with anticipation. They watched and plotted until their leader let out another horrific howl that reverberated like an earthquake, the smaller demons swirling through the air, wings flapping to regain control.

"What are you waiting for, you idiots?" Bellian yowled. "GO!"

The room emptied in a chaotic motion. Each creature flew, slithered, hobbled, or ran to find their prey.

Chapter 1

KRYSTAL was relieved the screaming had finally stopped. But now her dad's side of the closet lay bare except for a few lonely clothes hangers. Would she ever see him again? She drew in a deep breath and turned away only to see his side of the bed was still made. She'd like to crawl in and breathe any scent of him that remained. On second thought, no. There would be no tears. They never helped anyone. She walked from her parents' bedroom and into her own. She needed to get dressed for school so she wouldn't be late.

The grinding of the blender from the kitchen burst through the morning's silent gloom and wrecked her unsettled nerves. Her mom was making the usual healthy breakfast smoothie. She decided to forgo the Pop-Tart from her secret stash and have one of those smoothies. Anything to help break her record at track practice today.

KRYSTAL threw her head back and thrust herself across the finish line. She bent over at the waist, breathing hard.

Coach Lopez gave her a little smack on the back. "Great job, girl!"

"What's my time?"

Coach glanced at her wrist. "Two minutes and thirty seconds, and that's an honorable time for the eight hundred meter. You're looking at scholarship opportunities at this point."

Krystal appreciated the compliment, especially coming from Coach. Sure, she was tough but actually really cool too. Krystal headed for the locker room. Her teammates' approving nods went unnoticed. The year-long goal, now achieved, faded like an old sweatshirt at the sight of herself in the mirror.

She dabbed her patchy red face, then pulled the band from her ponytail, critiquing the now mousy-brown color that used to be blonde as a child. Starting from the bottom, scrutinizing herself inch by inch, the laser focus paused on her legs. No matter how hard the training, her stupid dimpled baby doll knees gave her legs a cherub-like appearance. But worst yet, she had no boobs whatsoever.

Coach Lopez, on the other hand, had strong, sculpted legs and real breasts, not fake ones—Krystal could tell. Once, she'd seen Coach at the movies with a really cute guy, looking stunning in a beautiful dress, her long golden tresses draped over her bare, suntanned shoulders. She struggled to push her jealous thoughts away and headed for the shower.

Back in her clothes, she stopped by the vending machine just outside of the gym and grabbed a Snickers.

"Great place for one of these, right?"

Krystal spun around. *Oh, that voice.* "Hey, Bryce. I was just thinking the same thing."

He put a dollar in the machine. "How was practice?" he said, bending forward to grab his bag of chips.

She tilted her head to get a good look at him while he bent over. Bryce wasn't the same scrawny boy who tried to kiss her in sixth grade. She clutched her candy bar to her chest, quickly jerking her head up when Bryce turned to look at her with those gorgeous green eyes. His lips were moving, but his words were a mile away.

What would it be like to be kissed by those lips now?

Bryce put his hand on her shoulder. "You all right?" When there was no response, he waved his hand in front of her face. "You in there, Krystal?" He laughed.

Krystal adored his full and genuine laugh. "Oh ... uh, yeah."

Bryce's lips curved into his adorable little smirk. "Oh, yeah, *what?*"

She squinted, nibbling at some loose skin on her index finger. "Sorry. Guess I'm still excited about beating my record for the eight hundred meter."

"Okay, that explains all the cheering over there. You distracted me from my pitching, you know." He gave her a playful shove.

Often, baseball practice overlapped with track practice. Bryce in those tight baseball pants—now *that* was distracting.

"Well, excu-u-u-use me," she finally said, followed by an uncontrollable giggle.

Ugh! Every girl at school acted that way in his presence. *So obnoxious.*

Bryce chuckled and backed away slightly. "I gotta get back to the field and help clean up the equipment." He popped a chip in his mouth. "Congrats on beating your record. I'm proud of you, K." He held his hand up for a high five.

She smiled feebly, her hand smacking his. He flashed his million-dollar pearly whites, started a slow jog, and then turned back. "See ya later at the coffee shop, maybe?"

Even though they'd been friends and neighbors since grade school, things were different now. Back in sixth grade, he'd tried to kiss her and she'd pushed him away. Now, here she was wishing he *would* kiss her. Did he feel the same? There were times the possibility seemed real—when his eyes would lock with hers, staring momentarily before he'd grin and casually look away, only to do the same again.

Krystal wanted to say something but had no clue how to begin. *Hey, remember back in sixth grade when you tried to kiss me? Can we try that again?*

Lame. Totally lame.

As she looked down at her hands, she was still clutching the Snickers bar like an idiot. She opened the wrapper carefully but, of course, got chocolate stuck to her fingers. She licked them clean, then bit off a big, melted chunk. Chocolate always hit the spot.

After finishing her candy bar, she slinked through the restroom door like a cat. Empty. *Good.*

That is, empty to the human eye. Hovering in the corners of the restroom were hideous demonic creatures, waiting for opportunities to wreak devilish havoc. One of them stretched out its leathery wings and flew directly above Krystal. Its drooping arms and legs were like thin shoelaces, but its belly was bloated. When she opened a stall door, he skidded across the tile and grabbed hold of her legs, then anchored its talons into her ankles. She bent down and scratched. The little demon tilted its head to one side, avoiding her hand. Seeing nothing, Krystal straightened up.

She went into her usual stall. Squatting down to face the toilet, her ritual commenced while the pot-bellied demon, *Bulimia*, inched its way up her back, whispering in her ear. *No one will ever know. Hurry up and get rid of it!*

The rest of the motley bunch had moved overhead. They chanted and sent whispers into Krystal's subconscious. *You're too fat. You're ugly. You have legs like an elephant.*

She pulled her long hair back and stuck her finger down the back of her throat. The Snickers bar came up in just two tries. Wiping the saliva from her fingers with tissue, she flushed the toilet. The candy bar was definitely better going in than out, but still worth the effort. There was no way she could afford those calories. This satisfied the chocolate urge without worry.

Why then, was there always *guilt* afterward?

She went to the sink and washed her hands and around her mouth. Bulimia was still clutching to her shirt. It inched up to her shoulders, massaging her scalp with its long, yellowed claws, conjuring unwelcomed memories.

As she peered into the mirror, her mother's voice pierced her thoughts. "You may have carrots or an apple for a snack, Krystal, honey. Cookies make you fat." *What a thing to tell a six-year-old!* "And where did these come from anyway? I didn't buy them. Your father gave them to you, didn't he?"

Her question was rhetorical, of course. Her father *had* purchased them. Just one of the ridiculous things they'd fight about until the argument turned into a knock-down, drag-out, screaming match. Her mother's words were always more venomous, which usually resulted in her father walking out the door with hunched shoulders, looking at the floor.

Krystal shrugged the memories away and began to apply her lip gloss, but she heard something ... or was it *someone*? Pivoting on one foot, she turned around. The sound was coming from one of the stalls and echoed eerily throughout the tiled room, like crying or whimpering. The sound bounced off the walls and enveloped her. A chill rose up her back, causing her to shudder. She swatted at something that whooshed past her head—saw nothing. But she *felt* something. Like something was watching.

There's something evil in here.

The crying grew louder. To her relief, the sounds were definitely human. *What if whoever's in there knows what I just did?* The muffled cries continued while Krystal stood there, contemplating what to do.

The stall door opened to show the new girl on the track team. Mackenzie took one startled look at her and turned back into the stall shutting the door with a solid thud.

"Mackenzie? That's your name, right? Are you okay?" She forgot about any embarrassment.

"I jus ... want ... to be alone," the girl said through heaving sobs.

Krystal shrugged her shoulders and began walking out but for some reason, lingered at the door.

Again, the stall door opened. Mackenzie blinked her doe-like eyes. "It's okay, you can leave." She wiped her nose with one hand and waved Krystal off with the other.

"I can't. I'd feel too bad."

"You don't even know me, so how can you feel bad? And by the way, yes, my name *is* Mackenzie."

Krystal walked back to the sink. "Well, I don't *know* you, know you, but we are on the track team together."

"Yeah, I know. You're Krystal. Coach's favorite." Mackenzie had a little edge to her voice.

"What? That's crazy."

"Come on. I'm new, and even I can see that. I've heard the other girls talk about it too. Don't worry, I won't tell them about your little *problem.*"

"My *problem?*"

"I heard you throwing up. I was in here last week when you did the same thing." Mackenzie's sarcastic tone quickly turned to remorse. "Wow, I'm such a jerk. That was a totally mean thing to say."

Krystal just stood staring at Mackenzie, immobilized. She was always so careful to make sure no one was in the bathroom. This girl knew something about her that was craftily hidden for years behind her towering walls of protection. But those walls were now crumbling, leaving her naked and vulnerable with nowhere to hide.

Demons—*Shame, Embarrassment, Fear,* and *Confusion*—inched closer, their long nails clicking across the tiled floor. Krystal struggled for composure, but a lone tear trickled down her cheek against her will. The sturdy, two-headed demon, *Anger,* seized the opportunity and shoved past the others. One of its heads was much larger than the other which appeared to be almost shrunken until it inflated, growing at least four times larger. It made its way directly behind her, snorting sulfuric wisps from all four of its nostrils.

Mackenzie put her hand on Krystal's shoulder. "Oh, gosh. I'm so ... sorry."

At the feel of Mackenzie's touch, Krystal's tears halted. Her walls of protection were now back in place and even more fortified. Her shame and fear were replaced with a raging inferno.

She stepped forward within a few inches of Mackenzie's face. "Ya know what? You're right about one thing. You *are* a jerk!"

Mackenzie pulled her hand back, her voice trembled. "I won't tell anyone, I swear."

"Not if you know what's good for you." Krystal gave her a good, hard shove.

Mackenzie lost her footing and stumbled backward, landing on the floor against the wall.

Krystal glared down at her like a lion would look at its prey before an attack, allowing the threat to penetrate. Her pupils grew dark like soot, blotching out the usual warm chestnut color. Anger scaled up her back, egging her on.

"Just so we're clear. I. Don't. Have. A. Problem. But you sure will if you tell anyone. Got it?" She nudged Mackenzie's slumped shoulder with the toe of her shoe.

Mackenzie wrapped her arms around her knees, drawing them to her chest and nodded to the ground.

Satisfied, Krystal waltzed out of the bathroom, head held high like the track star she was.

Chapter 2

MACKENZIE remained on the dirty bathroom floor in utter defeat. The undetected sinister creatures hissed and chortled, hovering just above her.

Great, I've made enemies with the school's track star. The one thing I'm actually good at is running, and now I'm going to have to quit the team. I have zero friends, and this will just make it worse. I hate my life!

Tears returned to her pale cheeks. Here she was, hiding in the high school bathroom the way she used to hide in the bushes during recess in second grade to avoid the bullies. It was the same story everywhere they moved. Oh, why did her family have to move all the time? Thinking of her mother's condition, the answer was obvious. She just hated how it affected her.

You're pathetic. Get up and stop your sniveling!

One of the scrawnier demons waved its boney arms in an upward motion to assist Mackenzie to her feet. "Wait a minute. I know I'm a better runner than her. I beat her stupid record *last* year. Krystal ran 2:30? Well, I ran 2:25! I will *not* quit!"

With renewed confidence, Mackenzie practically stomped out of the bathroom. She rounded the corner, tripping over a baseball that rolled under her feet. Grabbing hold of the corner of the wall, she saved herself from falling, but scraped her hand and wrist.

A tall, dark-haired baseball player ran to her. "I'm so sorry. Are you okay?" He picked up his ball.

"I'm fine. Just wasn't expecting that."

He looked intently at Mackenzie making her feel somehow exposed, but at the same time, exhilarated. "Let me see your hand."

She let go of the wall and drew her injured hand slightly behind her hip, then slowly held it out for him to see.

He took hold of her wrist, tenderly examining the damage. Her heart fluttered. He smelled of freshly cut grass and his eyes were just as green.

"It's not a big deal. Just a scrape." Pulling her wrist free, she avoided his gaze.

"You're new here, right?"

Raising her head, she found herself captivated by the friendly, maybe even flirty, sideways grin that revealed a boyish dimple. "Uh, yeah."

Green Eyes held out his hand. "I'm Bryce Williams."

Reaching for his hand, she sputtered, "M-Mackenzie Stine."

The touch was electric. "Good to meet ya, Mackenzie Stine."

Her brain thought of words, but they didn't make it out. Instead, her quivering lips curved into a grin, her head bobbing up and down.

"Well, I'll see ya around school, I'm sure." He released his warm grip.

He turned and walked back to the ball field, glancing over his shoulder to smile at her again.

And just like that, Bryce Williams had shot an arrow directly into Mackenzie's heart.

Meandering toward the parking lot, Mackenzie pondered how there was something so familiar about him. Then it hit her. She'd known another Bryce Williams once. In fact, he was the ring leader of the second-grade bullies. He'd made fun of her Southern drawl and bony legs, calling her Scarecrow from Okieville.

The school had been terrible. Even the teacher was cruel. How could a seven-year-old be expected to know the capital of California when she'd only lived there a few weeks?

I knew the capital of Oklahoma though.

Mackenzie shrugged. Bryce probably just reminded her of Prince Charming. He seemed too perfect. No way could a guy like him be interested in her. Who was she fooling? But still, he was flirting with her. He didn't need to examine her hand, touching her softly as he glimpsed into her soul. He didn't need to turn back and smile at her, either.

Hmmm. She shrugged again, this time with a smile.

The day had been eventful to say the least. Things had gone from really, really bad to really, really good in only a few moments. While unlocking the door to her old Volkswagen, things took a turn once again when she spotted Krystal getting into the passenger's side of a minivan. The driver appeared to be her mother. A slow-motion scene from a movie playing out was her impression when the van passed in front of her at a snail's pace, all while Krystal's narrow, angry eyes shot daggers in Mackenzie's direction.

Turning over the ignition, the car sputtered and shook, like her recent false sense of confidence. When it finally started with a jolt, she headed out of the parking lot following directly behind the minivan. The van had on its blinker to make a right turn. Mackenzie also needed to turn right. She followed behind the van for a few miles until they finally made a left turn on a street only a few blocks from her house. Mackenzie wondered if Krystal realized she was following them. *Maybe she's worried about shoving me. Probably not.*

"Anybody home?" Mackenzie said.

As she heard a familiar impish voice from the back yard, her attention was drawn to the open sliding glass door. Her little brother was playing on the swing set, and there was her mother asleep on the couch—no surprise there.

When she stepped over the threshold to the back patio, her German shepherd, Bristol, jumped up on her legs, wagging his tail and panting his usual greeting.

Her eight-year-old brother, Del, caught sight of her. "Watch this, Mackenzie!" He jumped from the swing, landing face first into the grass.

She quickly ran to him. "Are you hurt?"

He rolled onto his side, scrunching his eyes tightly.

"Deli, talk to me." She knelt and reached out her hand before noticing a little smile developing across his lips.

Del screeched in delight. "Gotcha!"

Mackenzie tousled his overgrown curls. "What's Mom been doing?"

"When I got home she was on the couch, so I've just been playing." He shrugged. "Hey, she's up!" He pointed toward the door.

Her mother's voice sounded groggy. "Mackenzie, I need to talk to you."

"Yeah?"

Mom's house slippers scuffed, dragging her closer. "I need you to get supper ready tonight. I'm a bit out of sorts."

"After I go for a jog," Mackenzie said.

"Didn't you have practice? Isn't that enough running for today?"

Maybe you've done enough sleeping for today. "You *could* ask how practice was."

Her mother took a deep, laborious breath. "How was practice?"

"Well, let's see, I made enemies with the school's track star."

This seemed to draw her interest a bit. "Uh-oh. What happened?"

"It's a long story, but she ended up pushing me down." Immediately, Mackenzie wished she hadn't mentioned it.

"What? Did you report this to the coach?"

"Gosh, no. I don't need to." She grabbed Bristol's leash and mumbled under her breath, "I'm not in second grade." *Even though I acted like it today.*

Her mother's brows furrowed, and she gnawed her lip. "You just got back from practice. Maybe you should rest and have a snack." Her voice trailed off.

Mackenzie ignored her suggestion. Hooking the leash onto Bristol's collar, she slipped out the door.

A light breeze blew her dark hair back. She felt good to run freely, just Bristol and her—at least momentarily. Usually, running helped clear her mind. Helped free her from the responsibilities of being the oldest. Free from seeing her mother waste away on the couch. Free from trying to figure out what was wrong. Free from wondering if things would get bad enough for them to move ... again.

After running several blocks, she noticed another jogger ahead of her. The girl's posture and stride showed a true runner, not someone out for a quick little jog. As they approached the jogger, Bristol growled, lunging forward.

"What's the problem, boy?" She tightened her grip on the leash.

The other girl looked over her shoulder.

Mackenzie was shocked to see the jogger was actually Krystal.

"I have dog repellant, and I'll use it on that beast!" She said, rounding a corner to a cul-de-sac.

Mackenzie quickly followed suit. Bristol was happy to oblige, panting as he picked up the pace.

Krystal began sprinting.

Mackenzie wasn't going to let her get away and neither was Bristol. He was running so fast, her grip on the leash loosened. She reached her other hand, almost grabbing hold of Krystal's long ponytail that waved behind her like a proud banner.

What am I doing? Mackenzie came to her senses and to an immediate halt. Krystal kept right on sprinting ahead.

"Come on, boy. Let's go home." Bristol reluctantly obeyed but not before giving one final wrench in Krystal's direction.

She jogged sluggishly the rest of the way, contemplating what possessed her to chase after Krystal. Bristol seemed to realize that Krystal was a threat. His reaction made her brave, maybe? No. She'd also been out of character to speak to her mother sarcastically, especially knowing how emotionally fragile she'd become. Her mind went over and over the events of the day.

What's going on with me? Goosebumps formed on the back of her neck and down her arms. *I'm going to end up like mom if I keep on thinking like this. I need to think of something positive.* Her mind focused now only on his face and those ivory teeth and boyish dimples. Bryce Williams.

MACKENZIE put up Bristol's leash, filled his bowl with fresh water and sat down on the floor next to her faithful friend. Her *only* friend. "Come to think of it, boy, you are a good judge of character."

Chuckling at the thought of him growling and lunging at Krystal, she stood and opened the door for him to go out.

She opened the cabinet for a glass, but there were none. The sink overflowed with two days of dirty dishes. Shaking her head, she squirted soap into a cloth and began washing a glass. Her fifteen-year-old brother, Trey, came up behind her. "Are you making supper?"

"We don't have any clean dishes. What am I supposed to cook with?" Mackenzie retorted. "You need to wash these and have Harper dry and put them away. I'm going to take a shower. Then I'll figure out something to eat."

Trey opened the fridge. "Might want to order take-out. Your cooking stinks, and I don't think even an iron chef could make anything decent with what's in here."

Mackenzie chose to ignore his comment but only out of sheer exhaustion. She gulped down a glass of water, then headed for the bathroom, expecting to see her mother still on the couch. Instead, only a rumpled blanket lay on the armrest.

Walking down the long, narrow hallway that led to the master bedroom reminded her of a horror movie. The temperature seemed to drop ten degrees when she approached her parent's bedroom. The drapes were drawn, and her mother's curved outline lay beneath the comforter. What Mackenzie didn't know was tucked within the blankets with her mother was the pitch-colored, slithery, reptilian demon, *Depression*. And stretched over her head, its tail curled around her neck, was another black snake of a demon, *Suicide*.

Obviously, her mother had stopped taking her meds again. Had her father noticed? His job as a trucker seemed to keep him away more than home lately. She was beginning to think he liked things that way. Mackenzie choked down the lump developing in her throat, sighed, and quietly shut the door.

15

Chapter 3

TAMMI could feel her skin crawl at his touch. His fingertips were rough with calluses. The stench of his breath lay over her like a dirty sheet. She curled into a fetal position in hopes of disappearing or at least keeping him from his intentions. He pulled her hair away from her ear and rasped a putrid chuckle.

"You'll like this," he said.

No. Oh please, no.

She kicked and thrashed violently, freeing herself from the blanket that twisted around her legs, loosening the coiled grip of the invisible, dragon-like demon, *Incest*. She gasped for air, clawing at her throat. Incest had now wrapped its scaly tail around her neck. It knew she was nearly awake and wanted to keep the nightmare alive. It used its thick, stubby arms and legs for support while wrapping its tail tighter and tighter, hissing its long forked tongue into her ear.

"You like this-s-s-s." It mimicked her father's voice.

But it was too late.

"It was only a dream," she whispered to herself. "That's all. Only a dream."

Tammi brushed away the damp hair that stuck to her forehead and lay listless for several moments until the chills started and her teeth began to chatter. Like a child, she pulled the blankets back over herself creating a cocoon of safety. When the chattering subsided, words began to flow from her lips in a haunting melody. The timbre of her voice felt somehow consoling. The lyrics poured out of her like blood from a wound.

Grandma's voice cut through her song. "Tammi, honey?"

Peeling back the blanket just below her chin, she struggled to focus in the dimly lit room. She wanted to sit up, but a fat gargoyle demon—*Terror*—now sat on her stomach, straddling her sides, holding her prisoner.

Her grandma called out to her again, moving closer to the bed. "Tammi, are you all right?"

At the sound of Grandma's voice, Terror shuddered, loosened its grip and then slid down the side of the mattress, joining Incest under a far corner of the bed. There they would wait for another opportunity.

Her thoughts were jumbled, and her words came out that way too. "Bad ... dream."

Grandma sat beside her on the bed, praying silently. Beneath them, Terror curled into a tight ball, covering its knotted head with leathery wings while Incest writhed and winced. Grandma gently pulled the blanket back. "Do you want to tell me about it? Sometimes that helps."

Tammi had no intentions of ever telling Grandma. Her heart would break into a million pieces. No, she would never tell Grandma. Or anyone else.

"Maybe you don't want to." Grandma sighed. "It's okay. I think it would be good to get up and walk it off."

She sat up, enfolding Grandma's slight frame into a hug. Grandma kissed her head and stroked her long, wavy hair. Tammi breathed in her soothing, powdery-lavender smell.

"What do you say we take a stroll into the kitchen, and I'll make us something warm to drink?"

Perking up a bit, an idea came to mind. "Hot chocolate?"

Grandma rose from the bed. "I'll get it started."

Tammi looked at the clock on her nightstand. Four-thirty in the morning. She sat groggily for a moment, realizing it had been over a year since the last dream. *Why now?* When she was younger, it was the same dreams, over and over, night after night. After moving in with Grandma and Grandpa when high school started, the dreams began to dissipate.

Shuffling into the kitchen, she found her grandparents both sipping cocoa at the table.

"Well, well." Grandpa said. "You know us old folks like to get up with the chickens, but I don't think even the chickens are up yet, young lady."

She couldn't help but smile out of a deep sense of gratitude to be living with them. Why didn't they live closer when her mother died of leukemia? Then maybe her father would have never …

The awful thoughts melted away once she focused on Grandma, whose lips curved into a smile over the top of her mug. Tammi had her gray-colored eyes, but that's where the similarity ended. Grandma was short and ivory-skinned.

Tammi took after her mother's physique—tall, lanky even, but with warm caramel skin. She didn't know much about her mother's family—her other grandparents—only that they were African-American with skin like black coffee. Tammi looked more white than black, which seemed to be a problem. Several years had passed since she'd seen them last. In Tammi's mind, they were the grandparents who didn't want anything to do with her once her mother had died.

Tammi used to want to fit in but recently started to embrace her uniqueness and even the loneliness. The black kids at school didn't welcome her—not with those "freaky wolf eyes." The whites, Latinos, and Asians seemed to have their own cliques too. There was no one who cared but the two loving people who watched her from across the table, and they were all she needed, right?

Folding her hands under her chin, she now gazed into Grandpa's ice-blue eyes. They were like her father's, except Grandpa's had a twinkle of childlike innocence. Her father's, on the other hand, were cold and dead, with pupils like coal. There was something malevolent in them, like a demon would come and take over her father at times. Not wanting to believe in demons, but deep inside somehow she *knew*, and she was frightened to the core.

Chapter 4

SADIE held her breath, catching sight of the list hanging on Ms. Stapleton's door. A group of students were huddled in front, blocking her view. She stood on the toes of her four-inch heels, bobbing her head to catch a glimpse. No good. She couldn't see a darn thing. Only five-foot-two, she realized no matter how high her heels were, she wasn't going to be able to see.

Deciding to improvise, Sadie removed her shoes, turned sideways and maneuvered through the crowd until she stood front and center. Her baby blues danced quickly to the S column. Salazar, Shelton, Smith. She stared, relishing her new last name. There it was: Summers. She exhaled and squealed with delight. "I can't believe it! I got a lead dance role!" She said to no one in particular.

Now weaving back through the throng of students that peppered the hallway like carpenter ants, her thoughts were of gratitude. Miraculously, her "new" parents managed to get her into this private progressive school of fine arts and technology. Even though she'd been adopted for three years, she still had to pinch herself to believe this was her life.

After two years of living with her meth-head aunt and five more years in foster care, Sadie's hope of having a real family had almost dissolved. Yet she had always believed deep inside that God would get her to the right family. After all, the last thing her mother told her just before her death was, "Jesus will always take care of you."

Sadie pictured herself cocooned against her mother's lifeless body, listening to the clock tick rhythmically with the tree branches that scratched the window—screeeech, tick, screech, tick. A party streamer had rustled and come loose from the ceiling, releasing pink balloons that slowly descended to the floor. Her sixth birthday—the day that changed everything.

Oh, how Sadie had clung to her mother's precious last words. They served as her anchor when she felt lost and unloved, shuffled like an unwanted stray from one foster home to the next. In the last home, they called her "Annie."

"You think you're Annie and Daddy Warbucks is gonna come save you?" Her cruel foster mom poked Sadie's chest. Isabel would take her food away, her clothes away, and had even sent away the best friend she'd ever had.

But no one could take away Sadie's hope. And hope had not failed her. She was finally a part of a family—a good family—and was not going to screw it up.

Squinting from the glaring sunlight, she spotted the white van and began speed walking.

On her tiptoes again, she yelled into the open window, "I got a lead dance role!" Her mom clapped, bracelets clinking together in tune with her high-pitched voice. "Yay! I just knew you would!"

Sadie plopped into the front passenger seat.

Mom unbuckled her seatbelt and leaned over to hug Sadie. "I'm so proud of you, sweetie. Now, let's get you to dance class."

Dance had always been important. Her birth mother was a dancer too and had started Sadie in ballet at only four-years-old. Even then, the dream was becoming a dancer. Now here she was, the daughter of a graduate of the Juilliard School of Dance.

With her blonde hair and petite build, anyone who didn't know the Summers family would never guess Sadie was adopted. At least that's what Ming, her eighteen-year-old Chinese sister would say. This made her feel kind of bad since Ming was adopted as an infant and Sadie was still new to the family.

Ming didn't mean anything by it. From day one, she had welcomed Sadie and even shared her bedroom without complaining.

Their parents were a wonderful couple. Most of the time Sadie felt like the real biological daughter of Mike and Pam Summers. But she knew she was just a "mutt," like foster monster Isabel would tell her, "And no one ever wants a scrawny, dirty, skanky mutt."

The Summers had brought a dirty mutt into their clean, white, perfect lives. They put her into the bath like you would a rescued dog. They scrubbed and scrubbed, thinking she was clean. But some things could not be washed away.

"Sadie, you were born to be a dancer!" Heather, her dance instructor, said.

"So, I know this might sound craz, but what do you think the odds are of me getting into Juilliard like my mom?"

"Well, you're a natural." Heather tilted her head. "But it takes more than raw talent. It takes lots and lots of hard work that, honestly, most aren't willing to do. I'm talking about living and breathing dance and sacrificing most everything else. You need a professional coach."

Sadie knew more about sacrifice than Heather could possibly imagine. "I want to go to Juilliard," she said. "The way I figure, I could have a shot. I mean, what are the chances that I would get adopted by a graduate of my dream school?" Folding her arms across her chest, she continued. "I'm not afraid of hard work either." She moved a bit closer to Heather. "Will you help me?"

"I'm not going to lie to you, Sadie," Heather said. "You got a late start. And like I said, I'd recommend a professional coach, but your mom knows what it takes. Maybe if we all work on it together—"

The two turned to see Sadie's mom had slipped in.

"How long have you been here?" Sadie asked.

"Long enough."

"Will you help?"

Her mom's lips opened into a wide grin, exposing her perfectly straight teeth. "I've been thinking that I need to get back into shape, so I brought these." She swung her worn-looking ballet pointe shoes at Sadie. "Let's get started."

Chapter 5

SILAS shaded his face from the sun. A dark mass resembling a flock of birds blotched the otherwise clear sky. Squinting, he realized there was another mass following the first one. He furled open his celestial wings, shot upward and then disappeared. He followed the two dark masses as they made a downward spiral just behind the hills.

Thousands of evil spirits descended, spilling into the decrepit building's roof below like crude oil. Silas glided in and out with precision through the trees, landing just past the broken-down structure next to Philo and several other angels. They were dressed in full armor and clutched their silver swords that glimmered like hopeful beacons in the dank and foreboding forest.

Silas put his arm across his chest in a salute. "Your timing is impeccable as usual, Philo." He nodded toward the other angels.

Directly across from Philo stood Theo, a mammoth dark-skinned angel taller than the rest. His black hair was pulled into a knot at the back of his head. Silas had only fought in battle beside him once, but that was enough. He lowered his head in Theo's direction before speaking again to Philo.

"The enemy has aggressively increased in number, sir."

Philo nodded. "You were correct to send word to us, Silas. There's more at stake than the lives of the four girls."

Theo cleared his throat. "There always is."

"Are there new orders, sir? I'm at the Lord's service." Silas stood tall, his jaw locked.

Philo kicked a pinecone with the toe of his hobnail sandal and stepped toward Theo and Silas. The other angels, at least twenty, gathered closer. Their wings touched together creating a billowy circular barricade.

"Sunrise Church has also become part of the enemy's attack strategy. More specifically, Pastor Dave and his family; the youth pastor, Grant, and his wife; along with the family members of the girls Silas is protecting." Philo breathed deeply, his flaming eyes danced from angel to angel. "It seems a renewal of faith is springing forth and spilling out into this small town. Their prayers have reached the Almighty."

"Hence the despicable reinforcements," said Silas.

"Theo, you are assigned to Pastor Dave and his wife, Shirley. Silas, your orders remain the same—"

While Philo gave orders, cat-like eyes flickered yellow and orange in surrounding bushes. Gusts of wind howled through the trees overhead.

"Strength and glory to the Great I Am!" Philo's voice thundered and echoed through the forest.

The other angels shouted, "Amen! Glory to God!" Each raised their swords to the middle of their huddle. The clanging sounds sent the little demon spies into flight.

The spies from the forest slunk into a meeting already underway inside the bewitched Hotel Arcana. Bellian pounded its massive fists on the pulpit. "I want a full report!" The great horned beast's voice shook loose pieces of the already crumbling ceiling.

Misery looked to the others, motioning its knotted head toward Bellian. The others whimpered and trembled, shaking their heads from side to side. Misery snorted and slogged to the front. Someone had to make a report.

Anger muscled its way through the freakish horde, sending Misery and a few other smaller spirits swirling and shrieking through the air. The monster's second head grew larger with each step it took. Fear and Suicide slithered swiftly until they caught up with Anger, tightened a hold around its legs causing the beast to tumble to the ground with a thud just as he reached the pulpit.

Bellian's orange eyes smoldered. They rolled back into its skeletal head, releasing flames that grazed over the heads of the demons who had not yet ducked. "SHUT UP!" he bellowed, shaking loose more of the ceiling. The exposed pipes creaked, releasing a steady trickle of rusted water.

"This is as accurate of a report as any," Bellian said, looking down at Anger. "The Almighty has sent troops. And unlike *this* display," he glared at Anger, Fear, and Suicide, "they will work cohesively. What is the mission?"

"BONDAGE!" The room rumbled.

Bellian raised its fist in the air. "Keep them slaves to their past, their pain, their addictions, and afflictions!"

As Bellian spoke, a new energy surged through the musty basement. Howls, caws, and snorts reminiscent of the Amazon jungle reverberated, growing louder and louder.

"Remind them day and night how wretched and damaged they are. Keep them weak, angry, and hard-hearted. Go to them in their dreams. Keep them from peaceful rest. Stir up strife and division within their families and friends. Keep them isolated, feeling alone and miserable. Make them feel *worthless!*" Bellian's sinister laugh echoed above the discordant verve of the room. "Go raise HELL!"

MACKENZIE tried to slip past Krystal before practice. Of course, Krystal was surrounded by her usual posse outside the gym, and Mackenzie couldn't possibly get by unnoticed.

Bailey, a lanky sophomore, caught sight of her. She whispered something which drew the entire group's attention to Mackenzie.

Krystal scowled, flipped her long hair, and looked away.

Mackenzie rushed through the door, hearing them giggle as the door closed with a thud behind her. *Just great! Krystal told them about yesterday.*

Quickly changing into her running gear, she got out to the field before the rest. Starting her warm ups and stretches near the bleachers while keeping her back to the gym, she could hear the girls behind her. They were talking about Krystal and her record-beating time from yesterday.

"She's totally going to get a scholarship now," Bailey said from behind Mackenzie on her way to the track.

Mackenzie gritted her teeth but remained in her secluded warm-up routine, trying to appear unfazed by them. *I know I can beat Krystal's record. I did it before, and I can do it again.*

She had her right leg extended on the seat of the bleacher when someone knocked into her from behind.

"Oops," someone said sarcastically.

Mackenzie regained her balance and saw Krystal walking away, displaying a derisive grin only Mackenzie could see.

Coach Lopez blew her whistle. "All right, get warmed up and then we'll do our drills and strides."

As practice wore on, Mackenzie grew anxious with distracting thoughts of beating Krystal's record when Coach's whistle blew.

"Mackenzie Stine, I'm waiting."

She jogged to Coach. "Sorry."

"I'm working on a personal training plan for you," Coach said. "I read on your application for track that you ran 800 meters in 2:25?"

Mackenzie nodded to the dirt.

"Well, I'm excited to see that. We need another fast distance runner. Do you think you're ready to show me today?" Coach Lopez asked.

Mackenzie's stomach flipped. "Um, s-s-sure." Before she knew, they were at the track, Coach with a stopwatch in hand and Mackenzie with sweat dripping into her eyes. She wiped her face and concentrated on the orange cone markers.

Positioning herself, she waited for the sound of Coach's whistle and was off and running for her life. The focus was on one thing—beating Krystal! Head back and legs pumping, she ran like her clothes were on fire until she reached Coach.

"You weren't lying!" Coach Lopez yelled, holding the stopwatch in the air.

Mackenzie bent forward and gasped for air, noticing Bailey and a few other girls making their way to the track.

"What was her time?" Bailey asked.

Coach Lopez smiled. "It was *cheetah* time."

Mackenzie stood up straight, still breathing hard. "I'm guessing

2:27?"

"Guess again."

Krystal stood next to Coach Lopez, her lips pursed and arms folded across her chest.

"2:22!" Coach said emphatically, putting one arm around Mackenzie's shoulder and with the other, motioning for a reluctant Krystal to come closer. "This is so awesome, girls!" She looked from one to the other.

Mackenzie could feel Krystal's icy stare. Something in her decided to glare back. It was enough to see a glint of insecurity in Krystal's mocha-colored eyes.

Good.

Halfway to the gym, she heard someone call her name—Bailey, all smiles and jogging toward her, like they were best buddies or something. "Hey, you wanna go to the Grind with *us* later?"

"Who's us?" Mackenzie asked.

Bailey laughed deeply. "Oh, just whoever from track. It's kind of our Friday thing to do. Sometimes the boys' track and baseball teams show up too."

Alexis joined them. "You're new. You should come and meet people."

"Uh, maybe." Mackenzie headed for the showers.

"It's cool," Alexis called out to her. "We'll introduce you and stuff. Meet us there at 4:30."

I haven't said I'd go yet.

———

MACKENZIE took a deep breath, pausing in front of the coffee shop. The glass doors revealed several girls from track but no Krystal. *Yes!* She walked in hoping no one noticed her nervousness. Sweat was pooling in her armpits. Best to keep her arms close to her sides.

Bailey and Alexis waved her over. They'd joined at least three tables together. Everyone watched Mackenzie as she wove her way to their group.

"Sit here, Mackenzie." Bailey patted the seat beside her.

Pulling out the chair without lifting her arms too much wasn't easy. Her dark eyes scanned the table, taking inventory of who was there. The jazz music piped through the speakers, the blenders blended, the multiple conversations swirled around the room—then all faded when she caught sight of Bryce Williams at the end of the table. His gorgeous green eyes seemed to stare straight into her soul.

He tilted his head slightly, sporting an adorable sideways grin. She looked to Bailey thinking surely he was smiling at her. "Mackenzie Stine, we meet again," he said causing the several conversations at the table to lull.

She fidgeted with a straw wrapper. "Hi." Heat surged into her face, probably turning her cheeks blotchy red. *Dang it!*

Bailey's head spun quickly, her blonde hair swishing across her face. "Oh, you two have met?" Her voice rose an octave.

Gee, is it that surprising?

Bryce rose from his spot and made his way over to them. "You could say that. I nearly killed her with a baseball." He plopped down on the other side of Mackenzie.

The pools in her armpits were becoming rivers, her face probably looked like a cherry tomato, and she had no idea how to carry on a conversation with these people. Her mind went wild.

Why did I come here? They don't really like me. They just think it's cool that I beat Krystal. Wait until they see I can't even talk with them. They'll throw me away like last week's leftovers.

"Well, Mackenzie, this is Bryce. Bryce this is Mackenzie." Bailey giggled. "Oh, and Mackenzie just beat Krystal's time for the 800 meter. Coach called her a cheetah."

Bryce raised his thick dark brows. He put one elbow on the table and leaned in closer to Mackenzie. She caught a hint of his cologne, and the scent made her head spin.

"You *must* be a cheetah to beat K's time," he said. "Speaking of Krystal, I think that's her ordering a coffee."

Mackenzie's heart went into palpitations. She felt like someone turned on the heater making her afraid to lift her arms to wipe the tiny droplets of sweat that was forming on her forehead. This was getting to be too much. She was going to have an anxiety attack or something worse if she didn't think of an excuse to leave. *Maybe I am having an anxiety attack. Maybe I'm going to puke right into Bryce's lap!*

Her pocket vibrated. She stuffed her shaking hand in her jeans, pulling out the phone.

Oh, thank God. "Gotta take this," she told Bryce, then stood up. She walked toward the door. "Hello?"

"Where the heck are you?" her brother, Trey, said frantically. "Everyone is gone but Del. Why is he here all by himself?"

"Mom's not there?"

"I just told you *our little eight-year-old brother has been here alone!*"

"I'm on my way," she said, starting to leave, unaware Bryce had followed her outside.

"Everything okay?" He looked genuinely concerned.

"Uh, I'm not sure. I gotta go."

Before starting the engine, Mackenzie checked her text messages. Sure enough her sister, Harper, had texted asking why no one had picked her up. She texted Trey to let him know. Heading out of the parking lot, she noticed Bryce was still outside. Krystal had joined him and they were talking. Mackenzie watched while Krystal became agitated and started to walk away as he tried to pull her back.

Mackenzie wondered if they were a couple, but couldn't dwell on it.

All that was on her mind now was getting home. The last time something like this happened, her mom had been arrested and put in the hospital for a seventy-two-hour mental hold. They called it a 5150 in California. Of course, her dad didn't show up until after her mom had been in the hospital for three whole days. And what a surprise, he was on the road now. It was up to Mackenzie to figure things out.

She picked up Harper and tried to obey all basic speed laws to get home. As they turned the corner, they were greeted with the sight of an ambulance and fire truck in front of their house. A few neighbors gathered on the sidewalk. Emergency personnel were carrying someone out on a flat board.

The girls jumped out of the car and ran up the driveway. Trey came out the front door, holding Del in his arms.

"What happened, Trey?" Mackenzie asked.

"It's mom. I thought she was gone, but ... I found her ..." He looked at Del, obviously choosing his words carefully. "In the bathtub."

Mackenzie covered her face with her hands. She felt a hand on her shoulder—her father. He had tears in his eyes and looked as if he'd aged several years.

"Go in with your brothers and sister," he said with a cracked voice. I'll see to your mom. She'll be all right."

Mackenzie looked at him and then to the front yard where neighbors continued to gather. An attractive woman approached her father. "I'm your neighbor down the block, Shelly Williams. Is there anything my son and I can do?" She motioned behind her. *Bryce!* How did he get there so fast? Mackenzie had just left him at the coffee shop. She'd only taken an extra fifteen minutes to pick up Harper. Her head spun as Shelly continued. "I can run and get something for the kids to eat."

Dad shrugged his shoulders. "Thank you, ma'am," he said. "I can't think straight right now." He turned, leaving Shelly Williams and Bryce on the porch facing Mackenzie and her siblings.

Mackenzie looked away from the Williams to watch her dad getting into the front seat of the ambulance when Mrs. Williams grabbed her hand and held it tight. "I'm praying for your mother, sweetie," she said. "Bryce, why don't you go pick up some burgers, and I'll stay here with the kids."

Bryce nodded, making awkward eye contact with Mackenzie. She quickly looked back at his mother. "Mrs. Williams, thank you, but you don't have to stay." *Please just leave us alone.*

"Oh, I want to help," Mrs. Williams said, walking in the door. "Go on and get those burgers, Bryce."

With a warm smile, she waved Mackenzie and her siblings into the house.

Trey looked at Mackenzie quizzically over his shoulder.

She shrugged. *What was happening? Could this get any worse?*

Trey set Del on the worn tweed sofa. Mrs. Williams sat next to him. "Hi, sweetie. What's your name?"

Del didn't answer. He just looked down, his lower lip quivering.

Mrs. Williams grabbed a children's book from the end table. "The Indian in the Cupboard. This must be yours." She tugged a chain inside the lampshade. Dust bunnies danced in the beams of light.

"It's my new library book from school. I have to draw a picture and write a report," Del said in almost a whisper.

"Well, would it be okay if we read together while we wait for those burgers?"

Del nodded. Dirt and tears streaked his pudgy face.

Harper sat next to Mackenzie on the other sofa, and Trey sat in

Dad's overstuffed recliner. Mrs. Williams tucked her bobbed blonde hair behind her ears with her manicured nails and situated herself next to Del, cleared her voice and began to read. She was a good reader. Her voice was soothing and yet full of life when she read the speaking parts. Mackenzie could tell that Harper and even Trey enjoyed her reading too. Of course, it was still bizarre, all of them listening to a stranger read a child's book as they waited to find out if their mother was dead. But it was sort of pleasant irony, since Mrs. Williams was so *motherly.*

Mackenzie stood up. "I'll be right back."

She headed to the guest bathroom, walking in and right back out. For some reason, she felt drawn to her mother's room and kept walking down the long gloomy hallway. Her parents' room seemed darker and colder than usual.

Mackenzie attempted to switch on the light, but the bulb must have burned out. She ran her hand along the cool wall as a guide, taking short steps until she was near the bathroom. The snake-demon, Suicide, had slithered from under the bed and was right at her heels. Her heartbeat was thumping in her ears. She reached around the corner of the bathroom door frame, then finally found the light switch.

Suicide had entwined Mackenzie's feet, creating a strange woozy sensation. Cold sweat beaded on her forehead when her eyes focused on the rumpled bath mat and prescription bottles strewn across the floor. She quickly flipped the switch and shut the bathroom door, racing toward a small sliver of light that came from the hallway. Once out of the bedroom, she slowed her pace and attempted to compose herself before going back into the living room.

Mackenzie walked casually back in, glancing at the clock on the mantel. Was her mother at the hospital yet? She envisioned a doctor looking at a clock and pronouncing her mother dead while pulling a white sheet over her body. She shuddered and tried to focus on the story Mrs. Williams was reading. Bryce had been gone a half hour. Ugh, Bryce. Why did it have to be him?

Mackenzie glanced at Harper, noticing she had absentmindedly bit her nails to the quick and blood was trickling down one of her fingers.

Trey noticed too. "Are you a cannibal or something, Harper? Go wash your hands."

Mrs. Williams stopped reading and looked at Trey.

"You don't need to be such a jerk to her," Mackenzie said.

Trey started to say something, then stopped. "Sorry."

Harper clinched both hands into fists and stuck them under her legs, trying to hide what she had done to herself.

"You're gonna get blood on the sofa!" Trey said.

Harper's chest began to heave in and out. Mackenzie knew the dam was about to burst.

Mrs. Williams promptly put down the book and moved to Harper.

"Oh, honey," she said. "Let me see your hands."

Harper shook her head. "I'm f-f-fine."

Del got up from the other sofa. "What's wrong, Hah-pa?" He used to have trouble pronouncing her name, but he hadn't said her name that way in at least a year. "Are you sad like Mommy?"

Harper buried her head into Mrs. William's chest and let her hold her like a mother would her own child. Mackenzie clenched her jaw and held her breath. She had to stay strong. The doorbell rang, jolting her from her near breaking point.

Thank God.

Trey opened the door. Bryce walked in holding brown bags that filled the air with the aroma of fried food and onions. Mackenzie's stomach growled unwillingly.

"I wasn't sure what everyone would want on their burgers." Bryce sat the bags on the dining room table. "I ordered two just plain and the rest have the works."

Mackenzie walked into the kitchen to get paper plates. Bryce was looking at her sympathetically as he stepped closer and stood beside her. She didn't want or *need* his sympathy.

"I'm really sorry, Mackenzie."

Willing herself to be angry, she gazed forward and just nodded. No use—there was no way to be angry with him. But if she looked into those eyes, she'd surely lose it.

That. Could. Not. Happen.

Chapter 6

TAMMI awoke to the familiar strums of her grandpa's classical guitar. She stretched and rubbed her eyes, listening and admiring. Her father was an amazing guitarist too when he wasn't drunk, but his skill didn't compare to her grandpa. He truly was a master at his craft.

She threw on some sweats, grabbed her guitar, and followed the music into the den.

Her grandpa's eyes were closed as he played. If there really was a God, surely this music was inspired by him.

Each note bore deep into her body, pulsating through every vein and into her soul. Not wanting to disturb him, Tammi lingered in the doorway. That's when she felt a cold and tingly presence. The hair on her arms raised when out of the corner of her eye she caught a glimpse of a dark shadow as it zoomed beside her and upward. It was a familiar, haunting feeling she'd grown accustomed to but longed to be free of. Shuddering, she inched forward but still didn't fully enter the room.

Her grandpa began playing the song he'd been teaching her. Tammi took this as her cue. She sat quietly in a chair across from him and began playing. Grandpa smiled and nodded approvingly, eyes still closed. With the eerie presence gone, Tammi began to hum and then to sing the song about sweet grace.

Her grandpa joined, singing harmony. His voice was rich, bold, and smooth. Just hearing his voice, one would never guess he was a man in his seventies. The tone had a mystical quality that seemed to reach beyond her protective boundaries. How else could he get her to play and sing a spiritual song? She'd stopped believing in God shortly after her dad started using her as a wife.

Her grandpa strummed the last chord. "Tammi, that was much too purty to keep to ourselves." His eyes were moist. "How about you come to the music rehearsal and see what you think?"

He'd been telling her about the worship band at church. Every Thursday night he went to rehearsal, and Grandma went to her Bible study.

"I play at the coffee shop all the time, Grandpa."

"Oh, I know. And you do a beautiful job. Your grandma and I are so proud," he said, standing. "Well, I better shower and get ready for church."

"I thought church wasn't until 10:30."

"The band does a quick run-through before the service." He winked. "You can never get enough practice."

"Says the man who's been playing for over sixty-five years. Is there any hope for me?" she hollered as he strolled down the hall.

Tammi sat on her bed wondering what the band at her grandparent's church sounded like. Her grandparents would be pleased if she would finally attend. *What could it hurt to check it out? But if I go, they'd probably expect me to come back and then what?*

Looking through her closet for something church-appropriate, she found a dark skirt and blouse her grandma had recently bought her. The blouse covered the new ink on the top of her arm. That would make them happy. They never said they didn't like her tattoos and piercings, but disappointment showed on their faces. She got ready and headed toward the kitchen. Even blindfolded, she could just follow the aroma of bacon and coffee.

Grandma looked up from the newspaper. "That new blouse looks lovely. What's the occasion?"

"I thought I'd ride along with you to church," she said nonchalantly, pouring her coffee.

Tammi didn't look for their reaction but knew her grandparents were trying to be just as coy. They were never pushy about the church thing, but it had to be difficult for them. That she was pretty much anti-God and church wasn't a secret. Once she'd heard them praying for her about going. At first, she was infuriated but hearing the yearning and love in their prayers dissipated any anger. How could these two people have raised a monster like her father?

Tammi bit her lip and fidgeted in the back seat when they drove in the parking lot.

Why did I do this?

The church wasn't what she expected. It wasn't a holy-looking white building with a steeple and stained-glass windows. This was the parking lot of a mini mall complete with donut shop, cleaners, and thrift store. Next to the donut shop, there was a large banner that read, *Welcome to Sunrise Church* that had a picture of the sun between two purple hills.

The three of them no sooner entered the building when they were surrounded by half a dozen people. They smiled, hugged, and shook hands. Grandpa introduced her as his "lovely and talented granddaughter." A short white-haired woman, wearing way too much perfume, had tears when she looked at Tammi's grandparents then back at Tammi.

Tammi's lips quivered into a semi-smile. Her insides cringed when she caught sight of an enormous cross at the front of the room.

"Well, let's head on up to the front. Rehearsal starts soon." Her grandpa motioned ahead.

Tammi looked around as they walked. The walls were a mural painted a light blue color as the backdrop with the sun peeking between two hills just like the banner, but more elaborate. Rather than pews like the churches she'd seen on TV, there were folding chairs.

She sat in the front row looking at the makeshift stage while the band filtered in with their guitars, music, and coffee. Tammi was surprised to see her grandpa was the oldest band member. The pianist seemed to be in her thirties. The other guitarists looked barely out of high school, and the drummer had tattoos and wore flip-flops.

The music leader came down when he saw her. "You must be Tammi. Glad you came today. I'm Grant." He extended his hand. "I've heard what a talent you are." He nodded to Grandpa who shrugged his shoulders.

"Guilty as charged," Grandpa said, then put his arm around Tammi's shoulders. "Come up on stage, and I'll introduce you to the band."

After the uncomfortable formalities of introduction, Tammi slunk back to her chair and the band started the first song. A girl she recognized from school came and sat a few seats away from her, grinning from ear to ear. The girl stood, and then moved to the seat right next to her.

Oh, crap …

"I recognize you." Her voice was sweet like cotton candy. "I've heard *you* perform at the Grind. Are you going to be playing here?"

Tammi breathed out an obvious sigh, then put her hand at the back of her neck and rubbed and rubbed out a kink. "And you are?"

If the girl had a tail, she'd be wagging it like an excited puppy. "Oh, gosh. My name is Sadie. And you're Tammi, right?"

"Yeah, so?"

"So-o-o-o, will you be playing here?"

Sheesh, this girl can't take a hint.

"No," Tammi said flatly, looking up to see that her grandpa was watching her. He seemed pleased, and she didn't want to do anything to embarrass him. She'd better say more. "I just came to hear my grandpa play."

The girl wasn't fazed by her rudeness. "I think we go to the same high school."

"Yep." Tammi said. "Uh, are you like a cheerleader or something?"

Sadie giggled. "No, I'm a dancer."

Tammi grunted.

Sadie continued to smile despite Tammi's icy glare. "Well, I gotta get going. I'm supposed to teach a class of six-year-olds. So, I need to get the room ready."

Tammi jerked her head back. "Ew."

Sadie giggled again. "I love little kids."

Tammi's lip snarled. "Uh, why?"

"Because they are so adorable and sweet and fun." She grabbed her denim backpack, flipped it over her shoulder and stood.

Tammi rolled her eyes. "Okay, well good luck with that."

Sadie waved to the band and walked away, her long blonde curls bouncing as she exited around the side of the stage. Tammi raked her hands through her thick dark hair, exasperated by the whole encounter. Why was she here?

The band's rehearsal continued, and Tammi felt herself tapping her foot and wanting to grab her guitar. The music was much better than she thought church music would be. And the band members had a blast bantering back and forth with each other in between songs. Before long, the band had come together in a huddle near the middle of the stage, arms around each other's shoulders as Grant lead them in a prayer. *Yep, I knew something weird had to happen.*

After Grant's prayer, the band members dispersed in different directions.

Tammi's insides twisted when she noticed Grant heading in her direction along with the pianist. "Tammi, this is my wife, Lauren."

Lauren's brandy-colored eyes were warm and inviting. "So, Tammi, your grandpa has been talking about his talented granddaughter *forever*. I'm glad to finally meet you."

For some reason, she felt amazingly at ease and instantly connected with Lauren. "You're a great pianist. I'd love to have those amazing harmonies back me up." As soon as the words fell off her lips, Tammi wished she could take them back. *Sheesh, that was conceited.*

Lauren didn't seem bothered by her words. "That's funny, because I heard you play at the coffee shop a few weeks ago, and I love, love your voice! I'd be honored to sing with you."

Tammi felt her face getting warm. Compliments from anyone other than her grandparents didn't sit well with her. She always felt awkward and didn't know how to respond.

"No pressure, though. Let your grandpa know when you're ready. He has my number. Just text me."

Feeling more at ease, Tammi nodded. Sensing the service was soon to start, Lauren and Grant said goodbye. Her grandpa led her to the seats where Grandma usually sat during service and Tammi waited alone. She kept her head down, but she could hear people coming in, talking and greeting each other like a big reunion. Suddenly her nerves started up again. *I don't think I can tolerate listening to a sermon.*

Too late. She would have to suffer through the preaching for her grandparents' sake. She bit the loose skin at the sides of her nails and pulled off the black polish before her grandma sat beside her, putting her soft wrinkled hand on Tammi's, giving her a squeeze.

"How was rehearsal?"

"Actually, better than I thought it'd be."

Grandma gave Tammi's hand another squeeze then turned her attention to the stage. The lights lowered, and Lauren played an intro on the piano. Church was about to begin. There was no way out now.

Chapter 7

SILAS watched a steady flow of a tar-like substance ooze under the doors into Sunrise Church. In a blink, he withdrew from his rooftop vantage point and melted through the doors himself. He stood unnoticed at the back of the room. The ooze morphed into demons, dispersing in all directions like cockroaches. They slinked and slithered under chairs and into corners. A few even inched their way onto the stage, lurking around the instruments and behind the pulpit. As the pastor spoke, the demons sneered, baring their jagged teeth.

Something shiny to the right of the stage drew Silas' attention. There stood Theo, his eyes ablaze and his sword drawn. When the pastor lowered his head to pray, Theo lowered his massive sword slicing clean through a swarm of demons encircling the man. Their high-pitched screeches shrilled while they burst into a cloud. Theo sheathed his sword, gave an approving nod to Silas and vanished. The remaining demons morphed back into a dark liquid that retreated into every crack and crevice of the room.

The church service ended, but Silas walked in between the groups of people who stood around laughing, visiting, and making plans for lunch. He could smell the acrid stench of the remaining creatures as he made his way closer to the classrooms. He stopped at one of the doors, his hand on his sword.

SADIE had just finished scrubbing the crayon marks off the tables when her mom poked her head in the door with Sadie's younger brothers in tow.

"I just finished. Are we going to lunch?" Sadie asked.

Jeff, her ten-year-old brother, hollered. "We're going to lunch at Grant and Lauren's!"

Her other brother, Jake, who was nine, dropped his action figure while shoving past him into the room. Mom grabbed hold of Jake's arm. "Meet us at the car," she said, gently wrangling the boys out of the doorway.

"My Batman!" Jake pointed to the ground. Jeff gave it a kick into the hall.

Sadie smirked and shut the door, listening to her brother's laughter grow faint and disappear. She'd grown to love Grant and Lauren over the past year. The two of them probably knew more about her than anyone else. Of course, she didn't tell them *everything*. There were enough skeletons in her closet to fill a graveyard. No one needed to hear all of that. She didn't even remember most of her crappy childhood. There were more foster homes than fingers to count with. So, she'd stopped counting and tried to stop remembering. Who cares anyway? She was finally in a forever home.

Forever home—sounds a lot like a commercial for adopting a stray animal. That was her, right? *You're a skanky mutt. No one wants you.* The words sounded as if Isabel, her foster monster, *was* standing right next to her whispering in her gravelly I-smoke-five-packs-a-day voice.

Sadie didn't realize she was hearing a voice in her head, but not Isabel's. She was hearing the voice she'd been hearing since the night everything changed—the night of the fire. The voice belonged to the demon, *Abuse.* It and a few cohorts had become experts on Sadie's weaknesses and vulnerabilities. Today it lurked in shadows, waiting for opportunities to encroach on her thoughts with its subtle reminders. He would pluck her subconscious mind, playing the same dreadful dirge over and over. *Fear, Grief,* and *Lust* usually chimed in, composing a discordant symphony that played like a broken record deep in her mind. These miserable beings went to great lengths to destroy the influence of anything positive in her life.

Abuse stretched out its long, bony fingers, using its talons to massage Sadie's head, conjuring images from her past foster homes. Flashes of memories played in her mind like a horror movie. The others were moving closer when a bright spotlight beamed a protective barrier that forced them back. They frantically tumbled through the air, wings and gangly arms flailing. Abuse released its hold and flew backward as if it had been struck by lightning, then skidded down the wall where it lay quivering and convulsing. The other demons yelped like frightened dogs and joined Fear in the corner, cowering and shaking.

The bright light projected from Silas's eyes. He pointed his shimmering sword. "Go!"

The demons shrieked and shriveled into tight little balls. They disintegrated, leaving behind the pungent smell of rotten eggs.

Sadie pushed the awful thoughts away. She put her smile back on, turned out the light and shut the door, all the while humming "Jesus Loves Me."

Silas lowered his sword and hummed along until she left the room.

———————————————————

LAUREN and Grant lived in a welcoming cottage with a stone pathway lined with red and yellow rose bushes leading to a red front door. Their home reminded Sadie of a fairytale with the European windows and the usual smell of spices wafting from within.

The door opened, and Grant met them, beaming his toothpaste-commercial smile. The heavenly scent beckoned Sadie and her family to enter.

"Is that a roast I smell?" Sadie's dad, Mike, asked.

"Sure is. And it's just about ready," Lauren hollered from the kitchen.

Grant led them through French doors to a screened-in patio which was more spacious than their entire living room and kitchen combined. There were hanging plants, potted plants, and a fountain that made a pleasant tinkling sound. In the middle of the room sat the long table where many youth Bible studies had taken place. Today the top was covered with a crimson linen tablecloth and matching napkins.

Sadie knew the young couple didn't have a lot of money, but somehow they managed to put on a spread that felt regal. Glancing around the table at the people she loved most in the world made her feel safe. Her dad and Grant yammered on about sports. Her brothers picked at their food while playing some sort of game. And her mom and Lauren were chatting about recipes.

After the feast, Grant cleaned the kitchen while Lauren served coffee and homemade apple pie. A perfect meal accompanied by a perfect dessert served by perfect people. She bit her lip, looking at her reflection through a shiny pot. *Living with pedigrees doesn't make you one.*

Lauren asked Sadie a question, jolting her from her thoughts. "Sadie, how about you stay around and help me get ready for study tonight?"

"Okay, but it's not 'til six, right?"

Lauren smiled, "Yeah, but I figured we could just hang out a while, unless you have something else to do. Maybe homework or dance or something?"

Pam, Sadie's mom, adored Lauren. Sadie didn't even have to ask if it would be all right to stay. What else did she have going on? Today was Sunday, and the dance studio wasn't open. "No, I'm free."

"Great! I was thinking we could make some brownies for the study."

After Sadie's family left, Lauren began getting out the ingredients.

"Wouldn't it be easier to just go buy some snacks?" Sadie asked. "I mean you've been in this kitchen all day, Lauren."

"Ya know what? You're right!" Lauren tilted her head to one side. "Let's go buy some brownies. On the way back we can stop at the Grind for a latte."

Sadie smiled. "This is a way better plan."

Walking into the coffee shop was always a euphoric experience for Sadie. That initial aromatic burst of freshly brewed coffee mingling with the sweetness of sugar and vanilla tantalized her senses. There was only one expression she could vocalize, "Ahhh,"

"I know, right?" Lauren said. "Hey, I see a great table in the corner. I'm going to go grab the spot. Order me a grande vanilla latte and get whatever you want." She stuffed a ten-dollar bill into Sadie's hand.

Sadie stood in the long line looking around the crowded room when she noticed Tammi positioning herself on a stool up in the front. She was tuning her guitar when a lanky hipster guy with a goatee grabbed the mic.

"Hi there, people of the Grind," he announced in slow drawl. "I'm the new manager here, Pete, and it's my pleasure to introduce to you the *talented tunes of Tammi.*"

Tammi raised a pierced eyebrow, shaking her head slightly, then proceeded right into strumming her first tune. Pete nodded like a bobble head, walked backward a few steps and took a seat. When Tammi began to sing, a hush fell over the room. A guy Sadie recognized from school gawked, his mouth agape. Another table of kids stopped their chattering and turned their chairs to face the front. But Tammi didn't notice. Her eyes were closed, and the music flowed out of her mouth and fingertips naturally like breathing.

"What can I get for you today?" The barista asked, pulling Sadie from her thoughts.

She paid for the order and wove her way to the corner table. "She was at church today." Sadie nodded her head toward Tammi.

"Yeah, I know," Lauren said. "Grant and I talked to her after rehearsal. Wouldn't it be great to have her on the team? She's so talented."

"Uh, I wouldn't count on it."

"Why would you say that?" Lauren asked.

"I'm not sure how to say this." Sadie twisted the straw wrapper between her fingers. "Let's just say the girl's about as friendly as a snake."

Lauren's eyes grew wider. "So you know her?"

"Not really. She goes to my school. When I talked to her today, she ... never mind. I don't know her and I shouldn't talk about her like that. Sorry."

"Okay, let's talk about you. I never asked how long you've been dancing. I bet since you could walk, right?"

Sadie had a distinct memory of her real mama buying her first ballet shoes and pink leotard and going for ice cream afterward. Her mother was a dancer too. Her father was a giant of a man compared to Sadie's petite mother. He hated dancing. Sadie could hear his booming voice. "You'll never dance again!" Those were the last words she ever heard him speak.

"You okay, Sadie?" Lauren asked. "You seemed to leave me for a minute there."

Sadie drew in a deep breath. She really wanted to tell Lauren about her birth mother but didn't want to end up crying. "Oh, just trying to remember."

Lauren was too smart. Sadie could tell she was suspicious but didn't press. There was only care and concern on her face.

"I want to tell you something." Sadie cleared her throat and paused a moment. "My father, he ... he ..."

Sadie felt the tears welling up. She clutched her plastic cup, looking down. "He was awful."

Lauren reached across the table and touched Sadie's arm. "I'm so sorry."

"I'm pretty sure he set the fire that killed my mama. They said it was faulty wiring, but I think it was him. It was my birthday ..." Sadie's lower lip quivered. "When I went back to the apartment with my aunt, the only thing left was ash and rubble." Sadie had a faraway look. "Until I got placed with the Summers, of course." She forced a big toothy grin. "That's all I want to talk about right now."

"It's fine." Lauren gave Sadie's hand a gentle squeeze. "I want you to know that anytime you want to talk, I'm here to listen. And one other thing," she said, looking squarely at Sadie. "I feel like I should tell you something. My uncle was an abuser. I'm actually going to be speaking about it at youth group. Not to everyone, though. Just the girls. But I'm telling you this now because I don't want you to feel weird after you shared with me what you did."

Sadie frowned. "Why are you going to be talking about it?"

"I want to help other girls, Sadie."

Sadie looked away. How could sharing her secrets with a group of people possibly help?

She was relieved when Lauren changed the subject. They drank their lattes and talked about youth group, enjoying the music until Tammi took a break. Sadie's eyes locked with Tammi's from a table not far from theirs.

Lauren turned around catching sight of Tammi, then turned back to Sadie. "I should go talk to her. Actually, *we* should," she said rising. "You coming?"

Sadie knew it was the right thing to do and the perfect excuse to avoid any more conversation. For some reason, Lauren had a heart for people like Tammi.

The expression on Tammi's face reminded Sadie of one of those bristly feral cats behind the grocery store, watching Lauren and Sadie approach. But that didn't deter Sadie one bit.

Chapter 8

KRYSTAL fumbled around the nightstand in search of her phone. *Who'd be dumb enough to call so early? And on Sunday morning.* She looked at the time before answering. *Noon already?*

"Hel-lo?" Her voice crackled.

Bryce spoke quickly. "Krystal, don't hang up."

Click.

Buzz. Buzz. Buzz. Her phone vibrated the nightstand.

She answered through gritted teeth. "What?"

"Look, I know you're mad."

"Whatever gave you that idea?"

He sighed. "I need a favor. It's important."

Krystal pushed the hair from her face and sat up, flinging off the black and white checkerboard comforter. "What's wrong?" She could never stay mad at Bryce, even when they were kids. Besides, she was more hurt than mad. Well, more *jealous* actually. But she wasn't going to tell him that.

"My car won't start, and I need a ride to the hospital."

"Oh, my gosh! What happened?"

"Well, Friday after our little, uh, spat at the coffee shop, I was almost home when I saw a fire truck and ambulance out front of the new girl Mackenzie's house." He paused. "Oh, I forgot, you know her from track, right?"

Krystal's lip curled and she could feel the anger chugging up her throat when she let out a huff. "Yep. What about her?"

"It was terrible, Krystal. The entire neighborhood was standing around gawking while the paramedics put her mom in an ambulance." Bryce caught his breath then continued. "Anyway, my car won't start, and I want to go see if there's anything I can do. I walked over to her house, but no one answered."

Krystal's mind was on overload. She stared up at the glow-in-the-dark stars on her ceiling. How long had those been there? Since second grade?

"Krystal?"

"Oh, sorry." She couldn't think of anything better to say. "I'm still half-asleep," she lied. "So you need a ride *now*?"

"I'm coming over," he said. "I'll bring coffee to wake you up. I can't believe you're still in bed."

"Coffee? Make it a large espresso with—"

"I'm walking to your house, dummy."

Click.

Krystal glared at her phone as if it was something detestable then tossed it to the end of her bed. She threw one leg out, then the other, and stood rocking back and forth with her eyes closed.

I. Hate. Mornings.

She scuffed to her closet, wanting to look somewhat attractive, even if there wasn't time for a shower. She decided to wear her favorite jeans—the ones that made her butt look much smaller. What shirt? Ah, the snug-fitting Angel's baseball tee shirt Bryce had given her for her birthday was perfect. He loved the *Angels* and everything to do with baseball.

While putting on her mascara, she saw Bryce through her mirror, standing in her doorway. "Hey," he said holding a tumbler of coffee. "Your mom let me in. Are you ready?"

She spun around and grabbed the coffee, clutching it to her chest dramatically. "Oh, coffee, how I love thee."

Bryce rolled his eyes. "Come on. I'm kinda worried." His voice sounded strained. "You're ready enough." He pushed her toward the door.

"Sheesh. You're gonna make me spill this coffee all over my Angels shirt."

He wasn't amused. *Darn it.*

"I need to see my mom real quick. I'll meet you out there." She tossed him the keys. "You drive since you're all fired up to get there so fast."

Bryce caught the keys without saying a word and headed outside. Krystal went back upstairs to find her mom bent over the laundry hamper riffling through the clothes.

"Mom?"

She jerked up and spun around almost in one motion. "Oh, Krystal! You startled me," she said, holding her chest. She was dressed in a skirt and blouse indicating she'd been to church.

"Sorry. I just wanted to ask you if you heard an ambulance around here on Friday?"

"Yes, I did." She turned back to the hamper and began sorting clothes. "Your brothers said it was the next street over."

"There's a new girl on the track team. Bryce said her mother had to go to the hospital. I'm driving him there to check on them."

Mom lifted a pile of clothes. "That's nice of you two. Let me know if I can do anything." Before leaving the room, she turned back to Krystal. "I'm leaving soon to pick up your brothers. They went to lunch with friends after church. Text me if you need anything, though."

Krystal felt her gag reflex kick in when her mom mentioned church. She wasn't convinced of her mom's sudden interest in *religion*. It didn't make sense. Her mom had always said the idea of a God was for weak-minded people.

Her mom was acting way too jumpy, so Krystal followed, watching her clutch the dirty clothes. Mom proceeded into the laundry room and closed the door just as Krystal passed by. Something just seemed *off*—like she was hiding something. She shrugged, headed downstairs and opened the front door, lingering on the porch in thought.

Honk! Honk! Bryce rolled down the window and hollered. "What's the deal?"

Krystal waltzed over to the driver's side and leaned in. "Hey, how about you just take my car? I don't need to go."

"What? Mackenzie is your friend from track," he said, lowering his head, his eyes peering over the top of his sunglasses. "Plus, I feel weird enough. It'll help if you're there."

Krystal pushed his sunglasses back up with her index finger. "Okay, you big baby. She's not really my friend. But I'll go." She backed away from the window. "Right after I grab something from the house." She turned and ran before Bryce could complain.

Opening the door as quietly as possible, Krystal crept up the stairs to the laundry room. The door was now open. Her mom was nowhere in sight and the washing machine wasn't on. She glanced around the tiny room looking for the pile of clothes, but didn't see them. She opened the lid. There sat the dry clothes with no detergent. Krystal reached in and moved the clothes around—her hand touched something cold and hard. A bottle.

Krystal sighed and pulled the bottle out, staring at the decorative label with flying geese. Vodka? A hard lump formed in her throat. She blinked back a tear. On a wire shelf behind some plastic boxes, two jaundiced, cat-like eyes glared, relishing in her pain. Krystal shivered then shoved the bottle back where she found it and padded downstairs and out the door unnoticed.

They rode in silence for the first few minutes. Krystal looked at Bryce. His shoulders were tense, and he had a scowl that scrunched his dark brows together. He always chewed his gum like a cow chews cud, but today it was like it took all his concentration to do it.

Krystal broke the silence. "So, how do you know this Mackenzie?"

His brows relaxed a bit. "Uh, I actually just met her. I accidentally *tripped* her at school, and then she was at the Grind with your track friends yesterday."

Krystal threw her head back against the seat and laughed. "Seriously, you tripped her? Or do you think all girls just naturally *fall* for you?"

Bryce glanced at her then back to the road. "Yeah, well. You never did."

Krystal nearly choked on her coffee. She didn't know how to respond. She saw Bryce glance at her out of the corner of her eye. She stared straight out the windshield the rest of the way until Bryce pulled into a parking space.

"Do you even know where to go?" Krystal asked, ignoring whatever just happened.

"No, I'll just have to ask inside."

The parking lot was enormous. Even though Krystal was tall, she had a hard time keeping up with Bryce and his long strides. They walked/jogged most of the way in awkward silence. As they neared the gothic-looking entrance, Krystal couldn't stand it any longer. "Do you like her?"

"Who?"

"Queen Elizabeth," She hissed. "Mackenzie, stupid."

Bryce slowed his pace, tilting his head and squinting. "I barely know her."

"Well, why the heck are we here?"

Bryce led Krystal over to a bench near the automatic double doors. "Sit," he ordered. "We're here because it's the right thing to do, K."

Krystal shook her head. "You've changed. And I'm not sitting," she spouted. "You're in a hurry, remember?"

He rubbed the back of his neck. "Yes, but we need to talk a minute." He sat down, motioning his head for her to sit next to him. "We've both changed, Krystal."

Krystal interrupted. "It's like you've gone all Mr. Nice Guy. It's weird." She looked away and then back to him. "We used to pick on new kids like her."

"We're growing up. We'll be seniors next year, and then we'll be off to college."

"No, it's not that, Bryce." Her eyes narrowed. "You've changed since you started going to that church thing on Wednesday nights."

Bryce's jaw tightened. "What are you talking about?"

Krystal stood up. "Let's just go in."

"Okay, but you're the one acting different." He pulled her arm and made her sit back down. "You were all moody at the coffee shop yesterday. And what's your problem with church? Your mom and brothers go. How come you don't?"

"Yeah, my mom goes, all right." Krystal clenched her teeth. "She also hides vodka bottles in the laundry. A lot of good church is doing her!"

Krystal stood again and walked through the double doors leaving Bryce on the bench. She headed toward the information table when she saw Mackenzie stepping out of the elevator. Their eyes locked momentarily, then Mackenzie gazed past Krystal, and a thin smile began to emerge. Krystal turned and saw Bryce behind her. *Of course. Why else?*

Bryce walked around Krystal. "Hi. I went to your house, but no one answered. So ... uh ... I ... uh ... we—" He motioned his head to Krystal. "—came to see if you need anything."

Mackenzie's dark eyes darted back and forth between Krystal and Bryce. The elevator opened. Her brothers, sister, and father came out and stood beside her. Bryce walked closer, extending his hand, "Hello, sir, I'm Bryce." His voice echoed in the large lobby. "My mom, Shelly, met you Friday." He paused and looked her direction, still talking much too loudly. "This is Krystal. We go to school with Mackenzie." He sounded so polite and formal. Krystal forced a closed-mouth grin.

Mackenzie's dad looked worn, and his hand quivered as he reached to shake Bryce's. "Howard Stine. Thank you for coming."

"Is your wife doing all right?" Bryce asked.

"She needs to stay awhile, but she'll be okay." Mr. Stine nodded. "Well, I'm going to go get these kids some food."

Bryce turned his attention to Mackenzie. "Hey, Mackenzie, Krystal and I are probably going to go get something to eat, ya wanna go with us? Uh, if that's okay," Bryce looked from Mackenzie to her father.

Krystal gulped. What the heck was he thinking? This whole thing was so weird!

Mr. Stine put his arm around his daughter. "Why don't you go with your friends, Kenzie?"

Mackenzie looked at her father, mouth agape. "Um—" She looked at Krystal, her ebony-colored eyes beginning to fill with tears.

An impulsive sliver of charity tugged at Krystal's heart. She wanted to hate Mackenzie, but for some dumb reason she couldn't. "Yeah, you should come." Her voice was flat.

Bryce's head snapped in Krystal's direction. "Great. Let's get goin' then," he said, squinting at her.

The three walked through the double doors and out into the sunlight. Krystal looked at Mackenzie, who was looking at Bryce. Practically every girl at school had that look. She began to feel angry and regretted giving in to her momentary pity for this stupid girl. By the way Bryce was staring at Mackenzie, she was certain this wasn't going to end well.

Chapter 9

MACKENZIE felt like she'd swallowed a grapefruit. Her heart was beating too fast and she was probably only two seconds away from hyperventilation. She picked at the slice of pizza in front of her.

Bryce had his elbow on the table resting his chin on his fist. "So, Mackenzie, where'd you move here from?"

She chewed her lip, thinking of all the places her family had lived. Her mind shifted to the memory of the Bryce Williams who'd bullied her in second grade. He had green eyes too. This Bryce, the sexy and sweet guy staring across from her could never be like that. *Oh, no! I better think of something to say!*

Mackenzie sucked in air too quickly and began to cough. Her face turned a ripe tomato red while tears began to stream down her cheeks.

Bryce handed her a cup of water. "You all right?"

Mackenzie nodded and took a sip, but the liquid came trickling out her nose.

Krystal tossed a stack of napkins across the table. "Here." She huffed, rolling her eyes and shaking her head.

Mackenzie grabbed the napkins and stood up. "I'll be right back," she muttered between gasps, hearing Bryce admonish Krystal.

"Sheesh, way to make her feel more embarrassed," he said.

"Well, that was gross."

Mackenzie continued to listen while peeking around the corner from the restroom.

"We need to make her feel better, not worse. She's new here, and her mom is in the hospital and—"

"And she's just a poor, pitiful little damsel in distress that needs to be rescued by a big strong man," she said with a southern drawl, squeezing his firm bicep muscle.

"Jerk." He rose from the table.

"Where are you going?"

Bryce leaned down close to Krystal's face and let out a belch, like they used to do to each other in junior high, then turned and walked away.

Mackenzie came around the corner and smacked into Bryce.

"Oh my gosh!" he yelled. "I just keep hurting you."

"It's okay," she said to the floor. *Could this get any more awful?*

"Come on." Bryce put his arm around her shoulder. "Let's eat some pizza."

Mackenzie managed a smile. Bryce was so kind. How could he be friends, or whatever he was, with Krystal? He kept his arm around her as they made their way through the arcade area, passing a father playing Ms. Pac-Man with his young son and two teens playing air hockey.

As they approached the table, Mackenzie caught sight of Krystal's frozen stare. Bryce must have too, because his arm gently slipped off her shoulder. He sat next to Krystal, giving her a playful shove.

She didn't look amused. Mackenzie couldn't believe she was sitting across from this awful girl who had bullied her in the restroom only a few days ago. What would Bryce think about that? And what was the deal with the two of them? They didn't seem like they were a couple. Maybe they used to be. And maybe she still likes him.

Continuing to pick at her pizza, deep in her own thoughts, she realized Bryce was staring at her. She bit her lower lip, glancing between Bryce and Krystal.

"I'm really sorry about your mom," He said.

Krystal's brows furrowed a bit. "So, what actually happened to her?"

What was she supposed to say? *Oh, my mom's mentally ill and every now and then she tries to kill herself.*

Mackenzie took in a deep breath. "I ... I'm not really sure."

Krystal wasn't buying it. "That's weird."

"Well, I'm just glad she's going to be all right." Bryce seemed to sense that Mackenzie was hiding something but was kind enough to let her off the hook. "So, I heard the track team started calling you Cheetah."

Mackenzie widened her eyes. "What? I don't really know ..."

"Did you hear that, Krystal?" Bryce asked.

Krystal's back stiffened. "They did, huh?"

Mackenzie got out her phone and pretended to look at a text, sensing Krystal's usual glare.

"I probably better get home soon." She tried to sound casual.

Bryce stood. "I'm getting a refill." He grabbed their cups. "I'll be right back."

Krystal looked at Mackenzie's plate. "You barely ate anything and we haven't been here that long, so what's the big hurry? Besides, you didn't answer my question."

Mackenzie repositioned herself at the table, then began scrolling through the texts on her phone. Anything to avoid eye contact.

"So-o-o, about the other day," Krystal mumbled.

Mackenzie looked up from her phone and then right back down. Her heart was pounding so hard Krystal could probably hear it. But then something occurred to her. *Krystal was nervous.* The only reason Mackenzie could think of was that she didn't want Bryce to know what happened in the restroom the other day.

Krystal fiddled with a napkin, shredding the corner. "I, um ..."

Mackenzie interrupted. "What, you feel bad now?" As soon as the words came out, she wanted to take them back. But it was too late. *Oh gosh, what have I started?*

Krystal's face grew flushed and her jaw tightened. She was about to say something when Bryce came strolling back to the table with the sodas.

"So, what'd I miss?" He asked.

"Not much," Krystal said.

Mackenzie sensed Krystal's vulnerability. "*Really?* You don't want to tell him about the other day?"

Krystal slouched in her seat. Her eyes widened, practically begging Mackenzie to stop. Bryce turned and looked at Krystal. "What was the other day?" he asked.

Mackenzie looked into Krystal's eyes. *She was scared. Good!* Mackenzie hesitated, toying with Krystal like a cat with a bug. "Oh, we were just talking about me being called Cheetah because I beat her record for the 800 the other day."

Krystal sat with her mouth agape and silent. Bryce looked at her and then back to Mackenzie. "Okay, now I *know* I missed something. What's with you two?"

Chapter 10

TAMMI exhaled an exaggerated breath when she saw Lauren and the *way-too-perky* Sadie making their way to her table. Sadie was beaming and spoke to Tammi from across a crowded table of hipsters. Her high-pitched voice squealed loud enough to be heard over the blenders, music, and talking, but Tammi shrugged and pointed to her ears. This only made Sadie laugh and repeat her sentence even louder.

"Oh my gosh, that was beautiful! You're so talented!" She exclaimed, drawing the attention of everyone within earshot, plopping in the seat right next to Tammi.

Lauren came and stood behind Sadie. "Hi, Tammi. Do you mind if we sit down?" She gave Sadie a playful shove.

Tammi grinned at Lauren's humor. "Sure, thanks for *asking*."

Sadie giggled.

Ugh, why is she so cheery? It's freakin' annoying!

"Sadie's right, your music is amazing," Lauren said. "Just let me know when you'd like me to sing some harmonies. I'd be honored."

Tammi was the one who felt honored. Even though they had just met that morning, she had respect for Lauren, who was an excellent pianist as well as a gifted singer. She seemed to be *real*, unlike most of the phony Christians Tammi had met before. Also, Lauren had caramel-colored skin like hers, making Tammi think she might be part black, which was intriguing—especially since Grant was very white—*cracker* white. She wondered if their families had issues with their marriage the way her mother's family did. Tammi knew firsthand how difficult interracial relationships could be.

Nonetheless, Grant was a talented musician, totally in love with his wife. Love showed in his pale blue eyes every time he looked at her. This also intrigued Tammi. The only other happily married people she knew were her grandparents.

Tammi realized her hesitated response to Lauren. "Oh. Um, thanks for saying that." Looking down, she picked at the rip in her faded jeans, exposing part of a tattoo on her upper thigh. She wanted to say more but couldn't think of how to phrase it without sounding stupid.

Lauren nodded. "Just telling the truth. And I mean it about singing with you."

"So, how long have you been playing and singing?" Sadie asked.

"I've been singing as long as I can remember and playing guitar since I was about five. My dad played in bars, and as you know, my grandpa is an awesome guitarist," Tammi said. "Why are you guys here anyway?" She continued to pick at the tear in her jeans, showing more of her brown skin and tattoo.

Sadie seemed puzzled or distracted—or both.

Tammi figured she was most likely trying to sneak a peek at her tattoo without being obvious but was about as subtle as a hurricane.

Sadie attempted to speak at the same time as Lauren. "Oh, sorry," she giggled. "Go ahead."

Lauren smiled at Sadie and shook her head.

Tammi sighed and rubbed her temple, toying with her eyebrow ring absentmindedly.

Sadie seemed to lose some of her bubbliness. Maybe she was finally getting a clue how obnoxious she was acting. Or maybe Sadie was distracted at Tammi's eyebrow jewelry that she was now purposely twisting between her fingers while glaring at Sadie.

Sadie cocked her head to one side, watching Tammi's fingers. "We're just hanging out," her voice went down at least an octave.

Lauren took the conversation from there. "We stopped for coffee before youth group at my house tonight. Hey, you should stop by. You can meet some of the other musicians from the youth band."

That got Tammi's attention. "*Youth* band?"

"Yeah, after group, there's usually four or five kids who hang out to practice."

Sadie instantly regained her composure. "Oh!" She chimed in. "I bet you know some of them. They go to our school."

Lauren nodded and got out her phone. "Want to give me your phone number, and I'll text you my address?"

Tammi fidgeted in her seat. "Uh, I don't know ..."

"Well, I'll send you the address just in case. So, what's the number?"

Tammi rattled it off almost under her breath.

Lauren's fingers typed quickly. "Okay."

Tammi's phone vibrated. She clutched the phone in her slender fingers, hesitating slightly before swiping the screen to read Lauren's text. "Thanks." She didn't look up from the phone. "Not sure that I'll come, though," she mumbled.

"If not tonight, we have it every Sunday at six," Lauren said. "No pressure."

Tammi was getting antsy.

Lauren could probably tell. "Okay, we'd better get going."

They rose from the table.

"Oh, here," Lauren pulled a CD from her bag and handed it to Tammi. "You may like this. The worship band made it over the summer."

"That's cool. I'll listen to it in the car." Tammi also stood up.

Sadie shot up from her seat like a firecracker. "I'll get us refills to go," she chirped, picking up their cups. No sooner had she taken a step, when she spun back around, blonde curls flying, and smacked the cups back on the table startling both Lauren and Tammi. "Hey, *you* should make a CD," Sadie said. "I'd buy it!" Then she picked up their cups again and left.

"Uh, okay then." Tammi said, grabbing her guitar case. "I gotta get going." She turned to leave then looked over her shoulder at Lauren. "Thanks."

Lauren smiled and waved.

Tammi raised her arm slightly, in an almost-wave, then left.

On the road, she mulled over the day's events. It'd been unique, to say the least. Now she was just tired. But not a physical tired—an emotional tired. She just wanted to put on sweatpants and crawl into bed.

And yet, something about the whole day felt ... *good.* Going to church hadn't been so bad. She felt uncomfortable meeting all the pristine-looking church people. They were not the judgmental bunch she was expecting—especially Grant and Lauren. Even Sadie's annoying friendliness was probably authentic.

But hiding on the floorboard lurked the dragon demon, Incest. It noted her lifted mood and began plotting ways to mess up her attitude. Much to the wretched creature's disappointment, Tammi remembered the CD Lauren had given her.

Aw, what the heck. I might as well listen.

As soon as the music began, Incest covered its tattered ears and drew further under the seat. Tammi listened intently, scrutinizing each note. *Not half bad.* The lyrics were kind of corny, but she found herself singing harmony by the second song. When the third song started, she could easily identify Lauren's voice. The ethereal tone stirred something within her. The tiny hairs on her arm raised when suddenly the CD skipped and stopped playing altogether.

Tammi gulped, holding her breath. Her car seemed to drop in temperature several degrees. Now the hairs on the back of her neck began to stand up, but not from the pleasant feeling from the music. No, she *knew* this unwelcome presence. She shuddered when the invisible beast moved its scaly claws over her ankle and up her calf, conjuring detestable memories of her father's calloused hands. She could faintly smell the stale smell of alcohol that usually accompanied him.

Tammi wished for escape. But how do you escape your own thoughts?

God, if you're real, please help me.

And just like that, Tammi could see Lauren's face in her mind as they spoke in the coffee shop and remembered her talking about brownies and youth group.

Pulling over to the side of the road, she stared at Lauren's text, made a U-turn, and headed the opposite direction from home.

Chapter 11

SILAS had been summoned by Tammi's prayer. Incest didn't have a chance once Silas's holy countenance illuminated the car. The small reptilian brute relented but vowed to return when another opportunity presented itself. And it would. Incest would make sure. But Incest wasn't looking forward to the lashing it would receive from Bellian after the report.

Incest slowly descended to the hotel's basement. A constant dripping of water echoed in the narrow hallway that lead to the conference room. Incest lingered with a few other dejected demons for their appointments with Bellian. A scrawny demon named Misery whimpered while two others poked and ridiculed.

"Your blunder has cost us all!" said Terror.

Misery covered its knotted head while the others took turns smacking it. Incest snorted and rolled its orange eyes. It didn't belong in the company of such imbeciles. It was a demon of higher rank and should not have to report every incident. But Bellian had new orders since the Almighty's angels had increased. Everyone had to report any sighting of the Almighty's army.

Incest jolted when the door to the conference room smacked open, rumbling the leaking pipes overhead. Anger flew, its two heads knocking together as it hit the wall, then skidded to the floor in a loathsome heap. Incest gulped and looked at the open door. No matter, it would hold up its dragon-like head high. It took large foreboding steps with all four legs, thick scaly tail swinging from side to side, hitting Misery. It flicked its forked tongue, picking up the smell of Fear and Agony. It gulped again but approached the pulpit, head still high.

Bellian glared down at the arrogant little demon but didn't say a word.

Incest cleared its throat. "The warrior angel, Silas, was sighted."

The dark slits down the center of Bellian's eyes grew wider. "Were you detected?"

"I'm not sure, your lordship."

"You know what I think?" Bellian didn't wait for a response. "My guess is the moment you saw him, you tucked that scaly tail between your fat legs and left!"

Incest lowered its head.

"Was he protecting the girl or only watching?" Bellian asked.

Incest kept its head down. "I was successful at diverting her attention from the disgusting music of the saints by conjuring memories of her father's abuse until she prayed, and Silas appeared in the car." Its voice was almost a mumble now.

"She *prayed*?" Bellian roared.

Incest heard a ringing in its ears. The impact sent the little brute skidding across the floor. Then all turned black. It tried to focus, but the room was spinning. It heard Bellian's roar once again and attempted to scramble to attention, back legs sliding in all directions.

"Go find the girl! She must not have even a sliver of hope in the power of prayer." It said. "Haunt her with nightmares. Tell her how disgusting she is. Tell her no one will ever want her. She is too damaged to be loved. Keep her so focused on herself that she forgets about prayer!"

Incest nodded its head and wobbled out of the room, passing by Anger who was still lying like a freakish blob on the cold, wet floor.

SADIE sat cross-legged on Grant and Lauren's tiny living room floor, twirling her long blonde curls between her fingers, while ten other girls listened to Lauren read a Scripture. The guys were in the backyard with Grant.

That's usually the way it went at youth group. All the kids would cram into Grant and Lauren's garden room for worship time and a short group lesson before dividing into boy and girl groups.

There was a knock at the front door. Sadie bounced up. "I'll get it," she looked to Lauren who nodded, continuing her sentence.

When she opened the door, Sadie couldn't contain her excitement and let out a squeal, causing those who weren't already turned around to do so.

"You came!" Unbelievable, the mysterious, drop-dead gorgeous, totally cool, totally edgy, extremely talented singer from the coffee shop was at *Bible study*!

OMG! Sadie couldn't resist giving Tammi a big hug, even though she had to stand on her tiptoes because Tammi had to be like six-feet tall, like a flippin' model for goodness sakes.

"Everyone, this is my *friend* Tammi." Sadie beamed. "She's a musician."

Sadie ignored that Tammi didn't reciprocate her hug, standing stiff like a mannequin. She even maintained her smile when Tammi raised her brows at being called her friend. For some reason, she was drawn to Tammi even though they were opposites in practically every way. Light—dark. Short—tall. Preppy—emo. Extrovert—introvert. The list was long. Sadie wondered if the others noticed how opposite they were. From the wide-eyed looks on their faces, she surmised they did.

Sure, Tammi had the bad-girl image down, but anyone who sings and plays like her must have some good deep down inside, right? Sadie was determined to find out. And once she'd set her mind to something, there was no going back.

She grabbed Tammi's limp-as-a-dead-fish hand and led her around the maze of girls that suddenly seemed very judging. Sadie figured they were just curious about her. "Come on over here. Pop a squat next to me." She sat down and patted the floor.

Lauren grinned at Sadie's enthusiasm then directed her attention to Tammi, who stood stiffly in front of her. "Glad you decided to come, Tammi."

Sadie watched Tammi's gray eyes dart around the room. Reluctantly, she sat down on the hardwood floor. Her thin shoulders hunched, wrapping her arms around her bony knees that poked through her ripped jeans. Sadie felt bad for staring and looked away, smoothing out her pink sweater with her petite hands. She just couldn't help herself, though. Tammi was an enigma she had to know more about. The fact that Tammi obviously disliked her just made her more determined. And for some reason, Tammi was at the Bible study! That *had* to mean something.

Lauren closed her Bible. "So guys." She let out a sigh. "Tonight I'm going to do something different. I'm going to tell you more about my testimony—my life."

Sadie's heart began to flutter, remembering the conversation they'd had at the coffee shop. *Oh, no! Was she going to actually talk about being abused as a child?*

Sadie squirmed, accidentally kicking Tammi, pushing her off balance. Tammi's head snapped in her direction. "Sorry," she whispered, leaning into Tammi's ear. Tammi sighed and then scooted a bit the other direction. Sadie scooched herself closer.

Tammi turned her head, slowly this time. "Ever heard of personal space?"

Sadie covered her mouth to quiet her nervous giggle.

Tammi rolled her eyes, drew her legs in tighter to her chest, then faced Lauren's direction again.

"I was nine-years-old when Uncle Todd, my dad's brother, came to live with us on our ranch. He had lost his job or something. My dad was really happy, because he had injured his back and needed someone to help," said Lauren.

"I loved helping Uncle Todd with the horses. We spent practically every day together. My mom said we were like two peas in a pod." Lauren took a shallow breath, then continued. "I'm not sure when things began to change. I just remember growing more and more uncomfortable with the way he would touch me. I didn't understand the touching was wrong, because I loved him so much. He was funny and always made time for me. I was so confused."

Sadie wiped the beads of sweat that were beginning to slide into her brows. Her mouth became watery, like she was going to be sick. She tried to focus on her hands that she gripped tightly in her lap, but continued to peek glances at Lauren. Why would Lauren put herself through this? Her mind began to flood with her own awful memories. She recalled a foster home where she'd shared a bedroom with four other girls and only two twin beds. Summertime and even with the windows open, the small room was a sauna and smelled of sweat. Each night, one of the boys from the home would sneak in their room and climb into a bed. Sadie knew that each girl silently hoped it wouldn't be their turn.

Sadie shuttered. *Oh, God, I don't want to remember this.*

"Guys, this isn't easy for me to talk about. But I know that what happened to me has happened to so many girls." Lauren's voice trailed off a bit.

Sadie felt Tammi's shoulder brush against hers, startling her from her thoughts.

"Sorry," Tammi whispered.

Sadie got the feeling that Tammi was just as uncomfortable as she was. "Why is she telling us this?" Sadie asked her softly.

Tammi's striking eyes stared directly into hers. "How should *I* know?"

Lauren continued. "As you've probably guessed, my uncle began sexually molesting me. And as I said, I was very confused. You see, even though somehow I knew what was happening was wrong, I still loved my uncle. He told me what we were doing had to be a secret. So I kept it to myself for over a year. And for over a year, he took advantage of my innocence, love, and confusion.

"Everything stopped the day my dad found my uncle and me in the barn. I was so ashamed. My parents sent me to counseling, but I never got rid of that dirty feeling I carried with me at all times." Lauren cleared her throat. "But then."—her face beamed— "my junior year at church summer camp, one of the speakers gave her testimony. And hers was just like mine."

Lauren re-situated herself. "I couldn't believe what I was hearing. I thought I was the only one." Sadie noticed Lauren glance at her then look away. "All the hiding and shame. All the anger and guilt. To make a long story short, for the first time, I gave my whole heart to Jesus. The guilt, shame, and even the anger became less and less.

Not overnight, but I can tell you that today, I am finally free!" Her tawny eyes sparkled.

Sadie blinked back tears, unaware that Tammi was doing the same, as were a few others.

"It's so quiet," Lauren said softly. "Maybe you're all wondering why I decided to tell you my story. Well, if that brave youth leader from summer camp had not told *her* story, I'm not sure what my life would be like." She wiped a tear from her cheek. "I want each of you to know that I'm always here, if you ever need to talk. About anything. I know how hard it is to find someone you can trust." Lauren placed her hands in her lap. "So, I know this is awkward, but does anyone want to ask me anything?"

Sadie felt the nausea rising again and wanted to run out of the room but didn't want to draw unwanted attention. The room was much too quiet. No one seemed to be breathing, much less speaking, when the silence was pierced.

"What happened to him? Your uncle?"

When Sadie realized the voice was Tammi's, she turned not just her head, but shifted her entire body toward her. *Why would she ask that? Oh, my goodness. I wonder if...*

"That's a good question," Lauren replied. "Well, he went to jail. I haven't seen him since the day my dad discovered us in the barn," she said. "But I've forgiven him."

Sadie could hear someone whispering in the back of the room.

Lauren looked in that direction. "Anything else you want to ask?"

The whispering stopped, and the room grew uncomfortably silent ... until the silence was broken once again.

"How?" Tammi asked.

"How did I forgive him?" Lauren asked.

Tammi nodded, and picked at the rips in her jeans.

"It wasn't easy. It kind of happened little by little as I got closer to God. Then one day, I asked God to take away my anger," Lauren said. "I realized, by staying angry, I was only hurting myself. It was like I was drinking poison and hoping that my uncle would die. It doesn't work that way, ya know?" Lauren asked.

Tammi shrugged, still picking at her jeans.

"Tammi, thanks for asking. I'm glad you're here." Lauren said, then directed her attention to the others. "So, I just want you to know that even though it was an awful thing that happened, God has used it for His good. I've been able to help others who were in situations like me. If you have other questions, or whatever, you can text or call." Lauren looked down at her phone and back up again. "Before we break for snacks, I'd like to pray. Unless there are any other questions or comments?"

No one said a peep, so Lauren began to pray.

Sadie's heartbeat got louder and louder, pushing Lauren's prayer into the background. Her fingers quivered while she picked at the pink nail polish and frayed skin around her cuticles. She had to get out! She gazed around the room, anxious to get up, only to find herself staring straight into Tammi's misty eyes that stared back into her own. Sadie paused, noticing Tammi's shaking hands as she picked at *her* nail polish. Sadie bit her lip, and quickly turned away from Tammi's gaze, knowing that something deeply concealed had been exposed in both their lives. Wiping her nose with her sleeve, Sadie hopped up, slipping into the hallway and out of sight.

She went into the bathroom, shut the door and locked it, then slid down on the tile floor drawing her knees to her chest. Burying her head, she began to sob.

Knock. Knock.

Sadie jumped up from the floor. "Gimme a minute."

Gazing at herself in the mirror, there was no hiding her tears—dang it! She splashed water on her face and patted it dry. Oh, if only she could get out without anyone seeing her!

"No problem. I'll use the other one," someone said.

Whew! Now alone, maybe she could pull herself together and call her mom to pick her up.

But she wasn't alone. Her demonic companions had been summoned to join her, relishing in her pain. Lust was directly behind her, looking up at her with one bulbous eye while the other watched Fear slink its way up the wall, switching off the light with its forked tongue.

Sadie stood frozen in the dark for a moment. She quickly grabbed her cell phone which lit up her reflection in the mirror. Her usual round, pale face and blue eyes now looked skeletal. Her eyes were sunken inky-black holes. The sight was terrifying, but not as much as what she thought she saw behind her!

She immediately slapped the light back on and flung the door open, smacking into Tammi who flew backward into the wall.

Chapter 12

KRYSTAL tried her best to watch Mackenzie through the rear-view mirror while driving. Mackenzie came across so unassuming, but after what happened at the pizza place, Krystal wasn't buying it. She'd misjudged and probably underestimated her. And why not?

Mackenzie had been a weak, wimpy baby that day after practice. But now it was like after beating Krystal's 800-meter record, she was suddenly becoming brave. Bryce seemed to be fooled too, and that was *really* getting under Krystal's skin.

Krystal noticed Mackenzie wore very little make-up. Not that she needed cosmetics. Her dark eyes with long lashes gave her an exotic look, softened by the freckles that danced across her narrow nose. Krystal gritted her teeth realizing why Bryce might find her attractive. But what he didn't know was Mackenzie wasn't so innocent. She was shy but wasn't weak by any means. And she was pretty cunning too—using Krystal's bullying as leverage. Her eyes darted from the mirror to the road when Mackenzie's chin cocked upward in her direction.

Bryce rested his hand on the back of Krystal's seat and turned around. "So, just let us know if you need anything, okay?" His deep voice sounded concerned. "Oh, I guess it would help if you knew how to reach us." He rattled off his number as Mackenzie typed it in her phone.

"What about yours?" Mackenzie asked Krystal through the mirror.

Krystal noticed the little smirk on her lips and the tone in which she asked but, of course, Bryce didn't. When she didn't speak up right away, Bryce gave it to her. *Big, dumb oaf!*

"My house is the next one," Mackenzie said, her thin lips curling upward.

Krystal parked in front of Mackenzie's house, leaving the motor running.

Bryce hopped out of the front seat and opened the back door for Mackenzie, who gazed at him with wide puppy-dog eyes.

You little faker! Heat surged up Krystal's neck and onto her face while she watched the two of them walk to the porch. Bryce treated her like a glass figurine, placing his hand on the small of her back. Watching him was sickening!

When he came back, he'd no sooner closed the car door before Krystal pulled away from the curb.

"Gee, Krystal, let me get all the way in."

"Oh, poor baby. You can walk from here if you don't like my driving."

Bryce didn't reply. In fact, he was completely silent for the two-block drive.

Krystal pulled into Bryce's driveway, next to his out-of-commission 1965 Ford Mustang.

Before she came to a complete stop, Bryce hopped out.

Krystal put her car in park and watched as he rounded the corner toward his house and out of sight. Her stomach tightened and her heart twisted, thinking of how mean she'd been to him lately. And for what? *Stupid Mackenzie!*

Krystal's foul mood dissipated at the sight of her father's car in her driveway. *Daddy!* She'd missed him so much. He hadn't been over in at least two weeks. Krystal locked her car and rushed toward the house, hopping over her brother's skateboard, the hedges scraping against her leg.

When she reached for the door, the sound of her father's voice caused her to hesitate. And then her mother's voice came a bit louder. Her father's voice, even louder again.

Hand hovering over the doorknob, Krystal froze. She wished she could go over to Bryce's. But no—thanks to Mackenzie! She opened the door, and the yelling rose several decibels.

Avoiding the kitchen where the voices bounced off the walls, she headed straight for her brothers' room. Kamron's and Kasey's backs were to her, sitting in their beanbag chairs wearing headphones and playing video games. She closed the door without them knowing she was ever there.

She trudged upstairs, glancing at the family pictures that decorated the walls all the way up. What happened? Once in her room, she locked the door. She promptly put in her earbuds and cranked up the music as loud as it would go, while reaching under her bed. She pulled out her *for-times-such-as-this* treat box and took off the lid. The chocolate aroma caused her mouth to water. She unwrapped the first mini candy bar, then another, and another until her lap was filled with shiny wrappers. Gathering them, she stood and caught sight of herself in the full-length mirror. *Disgusting!*

She knew what needed to be done. She went into the bathroom, knelt before her porcelain god and gave up her unholy offering. All the while her demonic companion, Bulimia, sat on the counter, its gangly legs swinging beneath its swollen belly as it whispered hateful thoughts into her ear. *You're ugly. Bryce could never like you. Mackenzie is rail thin and look at you!*

Buzz. Buzz. Buzz.

Krystal's phone vibrated on her nightstand. "Hello?"

"It's me," Bryce said. "Can you pick me up for school?"

"Sure, I'll be there soon."

When Krystal arrived, he approached her window, raking his hand through his hair. She rolled it down, he stuck his head in, and gently kissed her lips.

Ring! Ring! Ring! Her alarm jarred her awake. *It was only a dream.*

And it was Monday.

Throwing one leg out from under the blankets, then the other, she stood, weaving back and forth. *Mornings stink. Mondays stink. My life stinks.*

She shuffled to the shower. Upon returning to her room, she checked to see if Bryce had texted or called.

Nope.

She sluggishly finished getting ready and headed to the kitchen where her brothers were fighting over the last of the Frosted Flakes. This was a big deal since Mom was a nutritionist and rarely allowed cereal in the house, much less a sugar-laden one. Krystal pushed past their lanky, adolescent bodies and scuffed to the coffee pot. At least her mom allowed organic coffee. *Maybe there is a God. Yeah, right!*

"Are you two getting a ride or do I need to take you today?" she asked. The twins were sixteen, but only had their permits.

Their baritone voices spoke in harmony at the same time. "Got a ride."

Relieved, Krystal filled her travel mug, grabbed a banana, and headed for the door. On her way out, she caught a glimpse of her mother slowly making her way down the stairs. She paused to say goodbye, noticing that her mother looked ill.

Her mom was usually the epitome of health, but this morning her face was pasty white with dark circles and bags under her eyes.

"Mom?"

Her lips trembled into a strained grin. "Oh, have a good day, sweetie." She patted Krystal's shoulder and stepped off the last stair.

Krystal didn't know what to say or do. "Okay." She hesitated at the front door. "Uh, there's coffee …" She gently closed the door, feeling a pang deep in her chest.

Recalling the hidden vodka bottle from the other day, the pang grew into a hard rock as Anger followed her out the door. With each concerned thought toward her mother, Anger countered with a negative, malicious one until all Krystal could think was how phony her mother and her new-found religion was.

When making the turn from her cul-de-sac onto the tree-lined main street, she saw Bryce. She'd recognize those broad shoulders and familiar walk anywhere. He had a slight bounce in his step that was endearing to her. She pulled along the curb, rolling down the window. "Get in."

Bryce kept walking as if he didn't hear a thing.

"Oh come on, Bry." She rolled to a stop.

He kept walking.

Krystal stayed parked, watching him walk ahead, his back pack moving up and down slightly. After a moment, she drove up slowly beside him again and parked. This time he got in, still ignoring her.

After what seemed like forever, she finally spoke up. "Listen, Bryce, I'm really sorry for how mean I've been to you." She pulled into the school parking lot. "Aw, come on. Do I have to beg?" She glanced at him, but he stared straight ahead.

She parked, turned the motor off and turned to look at him again. The sight of his handsome face took her breath away. Even though his dark brows were kind of scrunched together, reminding her of a unibrow, he was still *so* darned adorable.

He gave a little snort. "Maybe we can talk later." He opened the door and threw one leg out. "I don't have time for drama right now." He shut the door.

"Drama?" She said out loud to nobody. "Like I'm just so much drama? What about little Miss 'Oh-my-mom's-in-the-hospital'? *That's* drama!"

Sulking, she sat in her car while Anger seized the opportunity and climbed from under the seat, clinging by its talons to her headrest. Its second head had inflated to double the size. Each head had one enormous amber-colored eye that bulged with each acrid breath it took. It spewed profane and hateful words into her subconscious.

Krystal gritted her teeth, noticing Mackenzie had pulled up next to her. And had the audacity to stare right back!

Chapter 13

MACKENZIE couldn't believe her luck—a parking space right next to Krystal. And bonus, she was in the car! *Great.* Mackenzie stared for a good long moment before grabbing her bag and getting out. To her surprise, Krystal was waiting with her usual scowl. *She could be pretty if she'd crack a smile!*

Krystal's voice was gruff as she moved close. "I don't know what kind of little game you're playing, but it's not going to work with Bryce." She pointed her finger.

"Do you know why they sell mints at Starbucks?" Mackenzie pulled a packet of mints from her pocket and shoved them into Krystal's chest.

Krystal quickly pushed the mints back, shoving her against the car. "I'm bigger, stronger, and *faster* than you." She huffed her disgusting breath in Mackenzie's face.

"Well, you've got the *bigger* part right," Mackenzie said a bit too weakly.

Oh, gosh, what am I doing?

Krystal's fist came hard and fast toward Mackenzie's head. She instinctively moved to one side, avoiding an impact.

"You have *serious* issues," Mackenzie tried not to sound scared, but her stupid voice came out shaky *and* squeaky. "And I'm going to report this and the bathroom incident to Coach as bullying!" She escaped Krystal's reach.

Krystal didn't come any closer but stood with both hands balled into tight fists, her chest heaving. "You would. You weak little coward. Watch your back!" She shoved her shoulder into Mackenzie's before walking away.

Mackenzie sucked in a deep breath and tucked her hair behind her ears. *What have I done?*

To her relief, she didn't see Krystal the rest of the day until track practice. Krystal kept her distance, but the few times their eyes met, her glower caused Mackenzie to quickly look away. She shrugged it off, using it as fuel to run faster and harder.

It worked too. Coach was all praises to Mackenzie after practice but didn't say one word to Krystal. *Good!*

Mackenzie decided not to say anything to Coach about Krystal's bullying. By the way Krystal lingered after practice, she obviously was fearful Mackenzie would squeal. Mackenzie thought it best to keep the bullying information tucked in her arsenal for a later time. At this point, as her father would say, let Krystal simmer in her own stew!

Before heading home, Mackenzie texted her dad to see if she needed to pick up her sister. Surprisingly, he texted back saying he'd already picked up all the siblings. He even asked what she wanted for dinner. Well, at least there was something to be a little happy about.

That emotion was fleeting as her thoughts turned to her mom. Was she coming home soon? She imagined her mother's frail body curled on her side, lying in her dark, cold dungeon of a bedroom, imprisoned by her own mind. What caused her mother to sink so low into depression? What kind of terror grabbed onto her, holding her hostage and away from her family?

When Mackenzie opened the front door, she was greeted with the aroma of what seemed like her mother's pot roast. Her family's voices were coming from the kitchen. Her heart leaped. She dropped her backpack and rushed toward the kitchen.

She heard her dad's voice. "Kenzie must be home."

Then there was an unfamiliar female voice. "Oh, good. Let's set the table."

Mackenzie stood in the entry to the kitchen, perplexed. Her dad noticed her before anyone else. "There's my girl," he said, smiling. "You remember Shelly Williams? She was kind enough to bring us dinner."

"Where's Mom?" Mackenzie asked flatly.

Her dad cleared his throat. "Well, the doctors have recommended your mom stay longer, honey. And they may move her to another facility to give her better care."

Mackenzie scanned the room for some indication to verify the knot in her stomach. Trey's face was like a blank canvas. Harper's face was streaked with tears. Del, quietly coloring at the table, seemed oblivious.

"Why does Mom have to stay?" Mackenzie asked.

Her dad walked closer. "She needs to get stronger, honey," he said softly, touching her shoulder. "Until then, we're going to do our best to hold this family together. I've already told my boss I need some time off."

Shelly gave a stir to something on the stove. "Well," she said. "I think this is all set. I'm going to leave it on low and you all can eat when you're ready." She grabbed her purse and headed toward the living room. "Just let us know if you need anything. You have my number."

"Let me walk you out." He followed her.

Shelly held up her hand. "No need. I'll let myself out. And please know, my family will be praying for you all."

Mackenzie watched her father from behind, seeing his head nod. When he turned around, his face showed a strained smile and glistening eyes. Despite it all, he still loved her mother. She was relieved he was attempting to face their problems this time rather than avoiding them like he had before.

After cleaning up the dinner dishes, Mackenzie looked for her sister who should've helped. Harper was in her bedroom, sitting on the floor looking at photo albums. "Look at this one." She glanced up, her limp hand holding a picture.

Mackenzie sat down, smiling. It was an old photo of their parents she'd never seen. In fact, she'd never seen this album. Based on their images in the picture, her parents were very young and happy. "Wow." Her fingers ran affectionately through Harper's waist-length hair.

Mackenzie laid the album to one side and noticed a piece of paper sticking out of it. "What's this?" It appeared to be a birth certificate. Scanning it, the names weren't familiar until she came to: Angela Ross. Her mother's maiden name.

Mackenzie thought at first it was her mother's birth certificate until noticing her mother's name was identified as the "Parent." She looked at the top line.

Name of Child: Dylan Lee Ross

"What is it?" Harper asked over Mackenzie's shoulder.

Mackenzie drew the certificate to her chest. "Oh, just old paperwork." She tried to sound nonchalant. "Where did you find this album anyway?"

Harper looked down at her hands in her lap. "It was in a box in mom's closet," she practically whispered.

"Why were you in her closet?" Mackenzie asked.

"I just wanted to smell her clothes." She looked up at Mackenzie. "I know it sounds weird, but her clothes smell like her."

Mackenzie leaned in close to Harper, kissed the top of her head, then picked up the album, still holding the certificate. "I guess I should put this back. Go dry the dishes, sis."

She took the album into her room and closed the door. She got down on the floor and rolled onto her stomach, taking out the certificate again. Who was this child, this Dylan with her mother's maiden name? Mackenzie zeroed in on the middle of the page.

Father: UNKNOWN

She scanned the document looking for the date and started doing the math. Her mother would have been only sixteen-years-old.

Her stomach got queasy as the reality hit her. There was a brother her parents never told her about. And the child didn't belong to her father. Her mother's depression was starting to make sense. A shiver crept up her spine when she saw something from the corner of her eye, like a shadow or something dark and fast. She lay still, holding her breath. Seeing nothing else, she opened the album and found another document. "Certificate of Death. Dylan Lee Ross." A whimper slipped from her quivering lips. The date showed the baby died only two weeks after his birth.

Her mother was only a year younger than Mackenzie when she had a baby. Now other things were piecing together, like her mother leaving home at seventeen, and the fact that Mackenzie had never met her mother's parents. Did they throw her out? Did they know about her and her siblings? How did the baby die? Who's the father?

With each question came that familiar and unwelcome presence looming closer and closer. Propping herself on her elbows, she looked around. There was no visible shadow, but she *felt* it. It drew as close as her breath until it finally consumed her. Anxiety had dug its long talons into her right leg while the thick, black claws of Oppression dug into her left. Oppression inched its way up her leg and sprawled its scaly, thick body over hers like a scratchy blanket.

She wanted to run, but her legs were paralyzed. Tears trickled down her cheek. *Get up!* But it was no use. Whatever evil was holding her hostage had a strong grip and would not let her escape.

Gasping for air from the pressure of the unholy beast, she managed to cry aloud, "Oh, God! Help me!"

Oppression flew against the wall, and Anxiety let out a shriek, slithering quickly under the bed. Silas stood over Mackenzie, his eyes beaming light that engulfed the room. She felt the release from her captivity and a sudden burst of warmth but had no idea what had just happened. All that mattered was she could run again. And that's exactly what she did.

SILAS stood near the glass double doors of Sunrise Church and watched Theo, Philo, and several other angels gather near the stage.

His body melted through the doors and glided swiftly to join his comrades.

"It's been reported Bellian has increased its army significantly," Philo said, acknowledging Silas' arrival with a nod. "Theo, have you noticed an increase of demonic coverage over the pastor and his family?"

Theo's chiseled jaw grew tight. "Indeed, but so have the prayers." His expression softened.

There were sporadic nods from the other angels.

"Yes," said the burly Jason.

"I've been summoned day and night by their prayers," reported Jonathon.

Philo drew in closer. "Their prayers are increasing, but we must help insure their faith in those prayers. They must know the Almighty loves them and hears them. However, God has given specific orders in regards to their protection, and we must adhere to those orders as always." Philo turned his attention to Silas. "I know the affection you have for the girls you have been assigned. But there will be attacks you are not to interfere with."

Silas spoke. "Tammi attended church and the youth meeting. I just returned from bringing God's answer to Mackenzie's prayer for help, sir. But I am in the service of the Almighty and will retreat as ordered and fight only when commanded." He looked intently into his commander's eyes.

Philo's lips turned upward slightly. "I have no reason to believe otherwise about you or any of the angels here. This is a warning from the Lord to prepare you and the rest of us. Certain events must happen in order to draw the people to the only power that will save them. We know the Lord does not enjoy the suffering of anyone."

"Are there specific orders for me then?" Silas asked.

Philo folded his arms across his breastplate. "Each of you will know in the proper time. You are to continue as is until then. As I said, be prepared to stand down when notified."

These orders were not unusual to the angels. Since the beginning of the creation of God's most treasured ones—the ones he breathed his very life into—the angels had carefully relied upon the Almighty's wisdom. It was by God's orders and his timing they would administer messages, help, encourage, battle, and … stand down. The angels took great joy in their responsibility to serve God and human beings. Just as their Creator, they took no pleasure in watching the suffering of the humans they had come to love. But their trust and devotion to God's divinity and ever unfolding plans always prevailed.

"Go in the name of the Lord," Philo said.

In a blinding flash, the room cleared. That is, except for one tiny demon. Misery cowered under the stage, taking notes to report to Lord Bellian.

Chapter 14

TAMMI sat at the kitchen table early Monday morning, sipping coffee while her grandparents read the newspaper. A ray of sunlight burst through Grandma's plant window, warming the cheerful little yellow kitchen. She breathed in the tantalizing aroma wafting from her mug and closed her eyes in contentment. Deep in thought, she didn't hear her grandpa speaking.

He looked at Grandma over the top of his paper. "I guess she's still dreaming in her bed," he jested.

"What, Grandpa?"

He put down the newspaper. "You were gone all day yesterday, and I didn't get to ask you how you enjoyed church."

"Oh." Tammi hesitated, giving careful thought to her words. "I was surprised. I mean, I can't say I liked it, but it was better than I thought."

"Well, that's pretty good," he said. "Just let us know if you want to try it out again. There are a lot of kids your age, and I hear they have a youth band." He winked.

"Yeah, Lauren told me about that. I saw her and this girl Sadie from school at the coffee shop when I was playing yesterday."

Her grandma's eyes lit up. "Oh, that's good. Lauren is a special young lady."

"She's really talented," Tammi said. "And yeah, I can see why you'd say that." She took another sip of coffee. "She invited me to youth group at her house, so I dropped by last night."

Her grandpa raised his bushy white eyebrows. "Well, that's really good news—"

Tammi interrupted. "Pun intended." She winked. "Ya know, Good News. Get it?"

Grandpa's eyes became tiny slits and his lips turned upward. "Sharp as a tack once she's had her coffee." He looked at Grandma then back at Tammi.

"So, it was an interesting experience," Tammi said. "Not sure if I'll go back, but I do really like Lauren. Grant seems pretty cool too."

Grandpa nodded his head. "Fair enough."

"Hey, do you guys know if Lauren is part black?"

"Mm-hm." Grandma swallowed her coffee. "I think you and Lauren have a lot in common, with music and other things."

You have no idea. Tammi thought of Lauren's testimony. She slipped away into her thoughts, recalling the strange events at Lauren's.

TAMMI stumbled backward, grasping at anything to regain her balance.

Sadie had bolted from Lauren's bathroom, colliding hard into her, painfully smashing her boobs.

"What the ... ?" Tammi gasped.

Sadie's eyes were enormous. "I'm so sorry," she said rushing past her.

Tammi clambered to her feet and headed after Sadie. The stupid girl drove her crazy, but she could tell Sadie was freaked out, and for some reason she wanted to help. But once Tammi made her way back into the living room, she didn't see her anywhere.

Lauren signaled for Tammi to come into the kitchen.

She reluctantly went in, still glancing around for Sadie.

"Tammi, this is Bryce Williams. He plays drums and bass." Lauren smiled to Bryce who was also smiling.

Gee, are they all this friendly? So annoying!

Bryce put out his hand. So formal! Tammi extended her hand, but only to her waist, making him reach.

"Hey, I've seen you before," he said. "Oh, I know. You play over at the Grind." He squinted, scrunching his dark brows together. "Yeah, that's it!"

Tammi loosened from his firm handshake then wiped her hand on her jeans. "Yep. I've played there for a while."

Lauren chimed in. "Sadie and I just heard her play this afternoon."

"Uh-huh, you sing some originals that are pretty impressive," Bryce said.

Lauren backed away. "I'll let you guys talk shop, then."

Tammi looked at Lauren, who was already walking in the other direction. Come back. I don't know how to talk to this church guy! She remembered Sadie. "Uh, I need to go look for my friend," she said. Did I just call Sadie my friend? Oh, well. Whatever.

"Who's your friend? I'll help you look."

Urrrr!

"Um, Sadie."

"That little pipsqueak?" Bryce asked, cocking his head to one side. "Yeah, it might be a challenge." He laughed. "But come on, I'll help you find her." He waved her out of the kitchen.

Tammi hung her head, but followed him anyway. How did I get into this?

They searched in every nook and cranny of Grant and Lauren's tiny house, but Sadie was nowhere to be found.

"I guess she took off." Bryce shrugged. "Sorry about that. But I'm here." He flashed his perfect teeth. "Let's go back in the kitchen and get a brownie before they're all gone."

"I don't think so," Tammi said. "I should get going."

Bryce leaned back, holding his hands dramatically to his chest. "What? You don't want to hang out with me?" He gave a sexy, sideways grin.

Oh, he's trouble.

Tammi raised one eyebrow. "Look, I'm new to this whole youth group thing," she said, her hands motioning quotation marks. "Do all Christian guys act super-friendly and helpful, but really they just wanna get in your pants?"

Bryce stood with his mouth agape, dumbstruck by Tammi's crass comment.

She reached her hand up to his chin and gently guided his mouth closed. "Don't worry church boy, I was only joking with you." She patted his cheek before walking outside.

The laughter of her grandparents drew Tammi back to Monday morning.

"She's really dazed this morning," Grandma chuckled.

"I'm sorry," Tammi blushed. "I guess I didn't get enough rest last night," She stood up. "Maybe I'll go lay down until I need to get ready for school."

She set the alarm on her phone, then curled up with a blanket in the overstuffed chair in the den. Grandma hadn't opened the curtains yet, giving the dark wood-paneled room a cave-like feel. Good. She could easily take a quick nap.

From behind the curtain, Incest watched and waited for her to fall asleep. When her eyelids began to flutter, the thick, scaly beast inched its stubby legs toward the chair, wagging its burly tail in pleasure. With much effort, the creature stood on its hefty back legs, using its tail for balance, then hoisted itself onto Tammi's lap where it conjured up images from her childhood.

She squirmed and kicked in her sleep while the beast's orange eyes glowed in delight.

Her alarm went off, jarring her from the dream. She instinctively flipped the blanket off, hurling Incest from its position. She couldn't remember her dream but shuddered, recognizing a maleficent presence that made her jump from the chair, swiping at her arms and legs as if she'd been covered in ants.

Grandma poked her head in the room. "I heard the alarm. Oh, good. You're up."

Tammi was relieved to see her. "Thanks." She pulled her grandma into a bear hug. Incest recoiled at the sight of them, disappearing into a wisp of smoke just above their heads.

"Tammi, you're not smoking, are you?" Grandma asked.

She released her embrace. "No. But I smell smoke too," she said, too freaked out to take offense.

"Smells like rotten eggs." Grandma scrunched up her nose. She opened the drapes, sending dust particles dancing through the bright beam of sunlight that now flooded the room. "I'm sorry I accused you, honey." She was walking around the room now, looking for the source of the smell.

"I don't smell it anymore, Gram." Tammi shrugged. "I've got to get ready for school."

Tammi left Grandma still walking around the room, sniffing, and raising her head like a hound dog. "Very strange …"

Tammi shook her head. You don't know the half of it.

Chapter 15

SADIE stared at the minute hand on the wall clock in algebra. She sat with an elbow on her desk, resting her chin on her fist. Her eyes grew heavier and heavier. She'd hardly slept after what happened at Lauren's.

The bell rang and her head jerked up. How was she supposed to make it through a two-hour dance lesson? She slung her satchel over her shoulder and had joined the throng of noisy teens in the hallway when her eyes locked with Tammi's, who was coming straight for her.

Tammi had on heavy, black eye makeup that emphasized the light gray color against her brown skin. She always looked like a Hot Topic model. "What happened to you?"

Sadie chewed at what was left of her pink nail polish, struggling for words. "I … I had to go. My mom picked me up."

"Uh, yeah. I know you left. I mean what happened when you came flying out of the bathroom?" Tammi looked down at her.

Sadie shrugged, avoiding eye contact, but could feel Tammi looking at her. "I know it was rude of me." She looked up to see Tammi's face actually looked concerned—for a moment.

"Whatever." Tammi brushed past her.

"Wait." She called after her.

Tammi turned, flipping her bangs from her face, glaring at Sadie. "Well?"

Does she know?

Sadie wanted to say something but was at a loss. There were too many skeletons stuffed in her closet. Opening the door would mean they'd all start tumbling out. Best to keep it shut.

"Uh, I'm glad you came."

Tammi frowned. "Oh, yeah, it seemed like it when you came flying out of the bathroom and then ran away from me."

"Sorry."

A glint of compassion was in Tammi's eyes. "Well, no biggie, I guess."

"Thanks. I hope you'll come back, though."

"*Tsk*, doubt it." Tammi sauntered away.

Sadie watched her tall, slim figure gracefully weave through the crowd. She was a head taller than most of the guys but oblivious to their gawking.

Sadie opened the double doors, immediately spotting her mom's van. What a relief. She just wanted to go home and pull the covers over her head but couldn't. There was dance practice. If she was going to get into Juilliard, daily practice was a must. Dancing usually helped get her mind off things anyway. It would be good. She opened the van door and greeted her mom with her best smile. No need to worry her.

Practice was grueling, but at least Sadie felt better. "Can we stop for ice cream?"

"We need dinner, Sadie." Her mom giggled. "Good thing you're naturally thin. Most ballerinas don't eat ice cream. Maybe after dinner, okay?"

Sadie smirked. "Sure."

Her mom glanced. "On second thought, why not just get one scoop. You probably burned off every calorie you've eaten today!"

"Yay!" Sadie clapped her hands.

They sat across from each other, savoring their chocolate brownie crunch scoops. Two more things they had in common: ice cream and chocolate. This was their favorite ice cream shop. The outside looked like a Victorian-style house. Inside, the walls and ceiling were painted candy-pink. There was a long bar with turquoise bar stools facing an enormous display case of desserts. They always sat at one of the little white tables with the chairs that had pink seat covers and heart-shaped backs.

Her mom let her pink spoon rest in the cup. "Sadie, I'd like it if you'd tell me what happened at youth group last night."

Sadie gulped a chunk of brownie. *Oh, what do I say?* "I don't know."

Her mom reached across the table, laying her manicured hand on Sadie's arm. "Lauren called me today, honey. She told me what she spoke about at group, her testimony."

Fear snaked its demonic presence into their mother-daughter ice cream date. It slithered through Sadie's long blonde curls, channeling memories to manipulate her into silence about her many skeletons.

Sadie looked at her ice cream, pushing it around with her spoon.

Her mind raced with awful images that made her blush to think about them. It felt like her brain was firing in a thousand directions. How could she convey one coherent thought to her mom with a war going on?

Besides, Sadie knew this loving woman would shatter like an expensive vase if she knew even a fraction of the ugly things from her past. And maybe worse, Sadie herself would shatter. No, she must hold it in to keep from breaking.

"It sounds like Lauren already told you," she said without looking up, nudging a nut with her spoon.

"Well, Lauren told me about her testimony, yes. And she also told me that you seemed very upset."

"Other people were upset too," Sadie said, her voice raising an octave. "I bet what happened to her upset you too."

Her mom took a deep breath, brushing her bangs away from her forehead.

"Oh, sweetie." She paused. "I want you to trust me."

Heat surged into Sadie's face. Her mom was looking at her with pity. She didn't want or need anyone's pity! She looked down at her mom's hand resting on her arm, then slowly pulled it off the table. Her mom's furrowed brows and glassy eyes put a lump in her throat.

"I'm sorry, Mom," Sadie whispered, a tear now sliding down her cheek.

Her mom pulled a tissue from her bag. "Here. I'm hoping there will be a time when you feel you can tell me what happened."

Sadie dabbed her tears and then blew her nose. "Why are you so sure that something bad happened to me?"

Her mom shrugged. "I just know."

"I'm happy now. Isn't that all that matters?"

"I wish it was that easy, honey. But unfortunately, most of us need to work through deep wounds by talking to someone."

Sadie's chocolate brownie crunch was beginning to coagulate in her stomach. "I feel sick," she said. "I need the restroom."

Sadie made it just in time. A few seconds later and chunks of chocolate brownie would've been all over the black and white tile of the ice cream shop.

After washing her hands and face, she looked at herself in the mirror. Her face was deathly pale, reminiscent of the terrifying experience at Lauren's. An icy chill came over her as she recalled seeing something behind her in the mirror.

Fear was now twisting its slithery black tail around her neck, causing her to weave back and forth. Its forked tongue licked the air, while its flattened head crept up her neck drawing closer to her ear.

Keep ssssilent, ssskanky mutt, it hissed.

Sadie turned and ran for the door, to find her mom standing only a few inches away. Sadie held her hands to her chest in surprise, then fell into her mother's open arms.

She held her, gently rubbing her hands on Sadie's back as she prayed. "Oh, Lord, please show me how to help my sweet daughter. Chase away her demons and heal her from the evil that has happened before you brought her to our family."

Fear fell to the floor and writhed in pain when Silas, summoned by the prayer, appeared in a cloud of glorious light. He towered over Sadie and her mother. Holding his massive arms overhead, he sent dozens of pernicious spirits flying and shrieking through the air.

He wrapped the mother and daughter in an invisible blanket of peace and vanished as quickly as he appeared.

Chapter 16

KRYSTAL stopped near the open door to Coach Lopez's locker room office after practice. She could hear Coach singing sickening praises to Mackenzie. This was usually when Coach would take time with Krystal—but not today. She felt like a discarded pair of old shoes thrown to the back of the closet. Even worse, Mackenzie had seen her craning to listen to their conversation. Heat surged into her face at Mackenzie's smug look.

Her anger subsided, giving way to a sinking feeling in the pit of her stomach when she realized Mackenzie could use this opportunity to talk to Coach about her so-called "bullying." The idea was ridiculous but still, this could mean trouble. Krystal shrugged, determined not to let it bother her. She quickly showered and dressed, deciding to stop by the ball field to see if Bryce needed a ride.

Even from a distance she knew which player he was. He was bent forward with both hands on his knees, rocking from foot to foot, ready for action. His hat shaded his eyes, but the way he lifted his head when she approached, indicated he'd caught a glimpse of her. Her insides trembled. She'd no sooner sat on the bleachers when the coach blew his whistle. All the players raced in and huddled near home plate, leaning in as he spoke.

Krystal played a quick game on her phone then glanced up. The coach was finished and Bryce was on his way. What a sight he was to behold! But like a scratch on a record—skrrreeek—her joy came to a halt when she saw the dismal look.

She tried to ignore it. "Thought you might need a ride."

He sat down next to her, pulling off his hat to wipe his forehead. "Joe's giving me a ride. But I was wondering if we can talk later?"

She chewed on her lip and nodded. "Okay." She stood, her stomach feeling like it hit the bleachers. "Call me later, I guess."

He grabbed her wrist. "I'm not avoiding you, Krystal." He looked up at her. "I just needed a ride home. I didn't know you'd ask."

"Sure, I get it," she said.

Bryce was still holding her wrist, making her feel all fluttery inside.

"Cool. Maybe we can hang out later."

"As opposed to what? *Not* hanging out?"

Whew! Even though he was still holding her wrist, driving her crazy, she managed to behave like her usual sarcastic self.

He smirked, giving her wrist a little shake as he let it loose. "I'll text you later."

Krystal cocked her head to one side, watching him jog ahead of her and into the locker room. *A sight to behold indeed!*

When Krystal got home, the house was eerily quiet. The blinds were still closed, making the room appear sullen and lonely. She thought how silence actually does have a sound. There was a difference between peaceful silence, when things are scary silent, or sad silent. The house felt both scary and sad silent now.

She opened the blinds; sunlight poured into the room. That was kind of better, but something still felt weird. The silence persisted.

Krystal switched on the TV. A blaring commercial now masked the heavy aura that occupied the room. Where were the twins and her mom?

Oh, sheesh, are they at the stupid church thing? No, it's Monday.

She went into the kitchen to grab a snack. Nothing looked tasty in the fridge. She remembered the cabinet above the stove where her brothers used to hide their treats from Mom. Krystal climbed on a chair and opened the cabinet. She moved the old blender and some other useless kitchen gadgets, expecting to find a box of Twinkies, but instead found a half-empty vodka bottle. She hopped down, and dumped what was left of the clear liquid into the sink, listening to the *glug—glug* sound with satisfaction.

Even though the TV could be heard from the other room, a heavy silence now consumed the kitchen. Numerous demonic creatures had moved in, looking for ways to keep her family crippled in darkness and despair. These little terrors had been summoned by their evil high priest, Bellian.

There had been a security breach when the mom, Kamron, and Kasey's hearts had become tender toward God while attending church. The new orders from the high priest were to amplify shame, guilt, and anger by punctuating each person's weaknesses and secrets. The plan was proving successful so far.

She decided to leave the vodka bottle in the sink—a message to her mother. No longer hungry, she left the kitchen empty-handed and empty-hearted. The hurt from seeing the bottle was now a tight ball in her chest.

Anger crawled onto her back as she stomped upstairs to her room. While she lay on her bed, it ran its gangly, wart-infested fingers through her silky brown hair, conjuring rancorous thoughts.

Krystal was wrenched from her dark thoughts by the vibrating of her phone. "Hello?"

Bryce!

"Hey, wanna go to the Grind?" He paused. "Uh, can you take us to the Grind?" He corrected himself.

Krystal chuckled. "Yeah. When?"

"Whenever."

Krystal sat up, pushing the hair from her face, looking at the time. "Be there soon." She hung up the phone, walked to her mirror and stared.

Bulimia attempted to balance its out-of-proportion body on top of the mirror, its spindly legs dropping beneath its belly.

"You're too big. Just look at the size of your legs." She huffed, squeezing her thighs hard enough to leave bruises.

Bulimia's mouth curled into a simpering grin, exposing its yellow jagged teeth. With her help, its job was so easy! Krystal grabbed her make-up bag and went into the bathroom. She brushed out her hair and pulled it back into a high ponytail, then dusted her face with blush and powder. She stepped back and examined herself. *That helped.*

Bryce opened the passenger side door and plopped in. "Hey," he said casually. "So, I was thinking maybe we could talk before we take off." He smelled like soap and aftershave.

Krystal was intoxicated by his fresh scent. "Uh, sure."

He raised his brows. "Well, what's up with you lately? I mean, I can tell something's bothering you. At first, I was ticked when you started acting so mean, but I know how you get when something's wrong."

Krystal's mind took off on a rollercoaster. Where to begin?

Bryce looked at her with those kind, patient eyes.

What if I just reached over and kissed him?

"Tell me about your mom." His voice halted her thoughts.

"What?"

Bryce laid his virile hand on Krystal's forearm and her heart began to race. "You said she's been drinking."

"Yep. I've found two hidden vodka bottles."

"Do your brothers know?"

Krystal shrugged.

"Okay, I'm confused. My mom says she's been going to church and a women's Bible study with her." Bryce grimaced. "It doesn't make sense."

"Well, whatever. She's been drinking, and fighting with my dad, and forgetting to go grocery shopping, and looking like death warmed over, and ..." Krystal felt a hot tear slide down her cheek.

Bryce brushed the tear away with his thumb, and drew her into his arms.

Krystal buried her head in his shoulder and put her arms around him. She just wanted to feel his full embrace, but the stupid armrest was in the way. Her chest heaved while drawing in staggered breaths of his heavenly redolence. His hand rested on her back, twirling his fingers through her ponytail. His breath was warm in her ear.

"I'm sorry, K," he whispered.

She didn't want to seem like a whining baby but knew the longer she was upset, the longer Bryce would hold her. Why not use some of

Mackenzie's weaselly tactics. Nope, she just couldn't do it. "Thanks for caring, Bry," she said, taking her arms from around his waist.

Bryce released his hold slightly, and looked into her eyes. "What can I do to help?"

Kiss me.

She squeezed her eyes shut, trying to hold back more obnoxious tears. It wasn't working. She turned her head into her shoulder. His arm moved from her waist to her face, lifting her chin up. She opened her eyes. *Mascara!* She probably looked like a deranged raccoon!

"I need tissue." She sniffed while reaching for her purse on the floor at his feet.

"I got it." His hand brushed against hers.

She rummaged, but couldn't find one tissue.

Bryce took a napkin he'd found in the car and softly wiped Krystal's face. She reached up and put her hand on his. "Why do you put up with me?"

"You don't know by now?" he asked.

"Bry, I need to tell you something. Something I've wanted to say for—" She stopped. His phone was vibrating.

He pulled the phone from his pocket. "It's Mackenzie," he said, then answered.

Krystal sighed and shook her head in disbelief. It was like they'd been driving sixty miles per hour and then suddenly had to brake! At least that's the way she felt, but Bryce was listening intently to that *weasel*—nodding, saying, "Uh-huh," and "Oh."

She backed away from him and resumed her driving position. She gritted her teeth and crumpled the napkin in her hand. She glanced over at Bryce, who was engrossed in whatever Mackenzie was saying, so she took the opportunity to fix her face.

"Well, Krystal and I will be at the Grind tonight, if you want to get out of the house, or I can bring your book after."

Krystal turned toward him and scowled.

He was oblivious. "Yeah, my mom likes to cook. Glad your family enjoyed the dinner. Okay, see you later then. I'll be praying for you and your family, Mackenzie." His voice was dripping with sap.

"Sorry about that," he said to Krystal, putting the phone back in his pocket. "What were you going to say to me?"

Krystal's mind was whirling again. *What was that little manipulator up to now?*

"Kry-y-y-stal-l-l," He said in a sing-song voice.

Not wanting to get into an argument over stupid Mackenzie again, Krystal simply said, "I guess, just ... *thanks.*" She'd probably missed her window of opportunity to tell him how she really felt anyway. "Thanks for always being here for me, and I'm sorry I've been such a jerk."

"You've had a lot to deal with since your dad left." Bryce laid his hand on hers, then gave it a squeeze. "I'm here for you, Krystal. Just talk to me instead of lashing out."

"Seems you're here for Mackenzie, too," Krystal said, instantly regretting it.

"Ya know, you two actually have a lot in common. Mackenzie said she'd tried your phone first before calling me."

Krystal pulled out her phone. Sure enough, there was a missed call. *Why would she be calling? Did she say something to Coach about the bullying after all?*

"Maybe we do," Krystal said.

"See? That's a better attitude," Bryce said. "She might come to the coffee shop later. You should get to know her."

"Oh, I plan to."

Chapter 17

SILAS took the scroll from Philo's hand, glancing behind him at Pastor Dave, who was kneeling alone in prayer at the altar. He scowled after reading and looked up at Philo, his beefy arm now limp at his side, still holding the unraveled parchment. He drew in a deep breath, and his armored chest expanded. A glimmering beam of light from above drew Silas' attention. Theo, followed by four other angels, materialized near them.

Philo handed each of the angels their scrolls. The church's auditorium was silent while the warriors read their orders. They finished simultaneously with the same expression Silas still held on his granite-like face.

Theo was the first to speak. "Well, things are heating up." His gravelly voice matched his piercing dark eyes.

Silas gritted his teeth. "Yes, it's heating up, and we are to stand down," he said through gritted teeth. "The Almighty has a plan and always knows the perfect timing, but I must admit, standing down takes more strength than the actual battle."

Philo put his hand on Silas' shoulder. "A battle *is* coming, my dear friend."

"And we will be ready!" Theo shouted, moving behind Pastor Dave, still deep in prayer.

The other angels joined the young pastor, whose eyes were closed tightly, tears streaming down his cheeks. He raised his arms to the heavens and began to sing. A warm glow like the rising of the sun fell over the room. As the pastor sang, the words rose above him like twinkling stars. The warriors dropped to their knees in worship of the Almighty God, their armor clanging against the tiled floor.

"We will be ready for the battle, indeed," Silas said.

MACKENZIE didn't want to call Bryce but her math book was left in Krystal's car on the way home from pizza, and the homework was due tomorrow.

At first she tried to call Krystal but thought better and hung up. Hopefully, she played it off with Bryce. He still seemed to be under the impression she and Krystal were track buddies.

Maybe I should go to the Grind and pick up my math book after all.

Getting out would help take her mind off the certificates in the old photo album. Besides, this was another opportunity to make Krystal suffer. She remembered the look on her face when Krystal saw her in Coach's office. Yes, she'd go just long enough to disturb Krystal's time with Bryce, grab a coffee and her math book, then leave.

She peered into her closet, strategically choosing an outfit that emphasized her long, lean figure. She added some barrel curls to her naturally thick, wavy hair and even applied eyeliner. She hadn't spent this long getting ready since last Christmas when their family went to church..

Pleased, she backed away from the mirror and into her brother, Trey. "Where're you goin' all fixed up?"

"Uh." She hesitated. "Just meeting a friend at a coffee shop to get my math book."

Trey chuckled. "*You* have friends?"

Mackenzie pushed past him and grabbed her purse. She could hear Trey following her into the living room.

"Hey, wait," he said. "I was only kidding. I want to go too."

She whirled around. "Seriously? Like I'd want to be seen with you!"

"I'm going, Kenzie. I need to get outta here." He begged. "Please, I won't bother you. I promise."

"I'm leaving *now*. I'm not waiting for you to go bathe yourself in Old Spice aftershave, or whatever it is you do." She walked toward the door and yelled over her shoulder. "Dad, I'll be back in an hour."

Trey was in the car thirty seconds after her.

She turned up the radio to mask the awkward silence in the car. She could see Trey playing air guitar in her peripheral vision. "Oh my gosh, don't sit near me when we get there, okay?"

Trey laughed. "I'm going to put my arm around you like I'm your boyfriend!"

"That's it! I'm turning around and taking you home."

"I wouldn't do that," he said, turning down the music. "Hey, Kenzie." His voice cracked. "Are you worried about Mom?"

Mackenzie glanced at him. "Yeah. I hate this."

"Me, too," Trey said. "At least Dad's around this time."

"Yeah, but that has me worried even more somehow. Especially since she's staying in the hospital longer. Maybe she's going to die, or they will want to put her in a mental institute forever."

Trey's voice quivered slightly. "I know. I've had all kinds of crazy thoughts."

Mackenzie spotted Krystal's car in the parking lot of the Grind. She parked a few spaces down, turned off the engine, then looked at her brother. "Trey, I don't care if you hang out with me. I'm just picking up a math book I left in a friend's car." *I can't believe I called Krystal my friend!*

It was kind of nice to walk into the coffee shop with someone, even if it was her fifteen-year-old brother. Unlike most guys his age, he didn't have a face full of zits and he was actually sort of attractive. His shoulder length jet-black hair and leather jacket made him look older.

Mackenzie looked around the room, finding Bryce at a back-corner table. He stood and waved her over.

Trey leaned into her ear. "Oh, it's the jock whose mom brought us dinner. No wonder you got all spruced up."

She gave him a little shove. "Sh-h-h."

"I'll go get my coffee so you can walk over there without embarrassment."

Mackenzie saw Bryce move two more chairs to the table. "It's okay. It might be easier if you're there," she said.

Bryce put out his hand to shake Trey's. "Hey, how's it goin', bro? Trey, right?"

He nodded. "Goin' all right."

Bryce turned his attention to Mackenzie. "Glad you came." He rubbed her arm, making her tingle all over.

Her attention was drawn to Krystal, glaring like a feral cat. *Here we go.*

Bryce motioned. "Have a seat, guys."

"I'll go order our drinks," Trey said.

"I'll go with you. We need refills." Bryce followed.

Mackenzie's heart plummeted to her stomach, but she had to appear strong. She sat down across from Krystal, flipped her thick dark curls, and crossed her arms. "I left my math book in your car."

Krystal huffed. "On purpose, I bet."

"Yeah, because I enjoy your pleasant company so much."

Krystal's eyes narrowed. "More like you enjoy Bryce's company."

"Well, I must admit, he's a lot nicer. He hasn't tried to slug me or push me down," Mackenzie said. "You, on the other hand, are a jealous bully."

Krystal's jaw tightened. "Jealous of what?"

Mackenzie leaned across the table. "Let's see. I'm faster and thinner than you. And it seems that Bryce likes what he sees." She sat back in her chair, again folding her arms across her chest. "Are you going to try to hit me again, right here in the coffee shop? What would Bryce think of that, hmm?"

It was obvious by Krystal's bulging eyes she was reaching her boiling point. "Why don't we settle this outside? Or are you afraid like you were that day in the bathroom?" She rose from her chair. "Whimpering on the disgusting floor."

Mackenzie felt her lunch was chugging its way up her throat. *Keep calm. You have the upper hand here.*

"What do we really need to settle, Krystal? I never wanted to be enemies with you. I know we got off on the wrong foot the day we met. Maybe you think I'm going to tell people that you make yourself throw up. I'm not interested in starting any rumors. I just want a track scholarship. That's all I'm interested in."

"Uh-huh, really. And what about Bryce?" Krystal sat back down.

Mackenzie shrugged.

This time it was Krystal leaning across the table. "Listen, I'm onto you, girlie. You may have him fooled with this little nice girl act—"

Mackenzie motioned her head that the guys were on their way back. Krystal's eyes darted to the side then back to Mackenzie. "You better watch yourself," she whispered.

Mackenzie whispered back. "If you try to bully me again, you bet I'll talk. Like I said, I don't *want* to be enemies." She smiled weakly, looking up at Bryce who sat down beside her instead of Krystal. *Score!*

Trey handed Mackenzie her drink and sat down on the other side of her. Krystal looked like she was sitting on something sharp until Bryce reached across the table, placing his hand on hers. "Doing okay?" he asked.

Mackenzie tried to hear Krystal's response, but it was drowned out as guitar music and singing started from the front of the coffee shop.

"Oh, cool," Bryce said loudly and pointed to the guitarist. "I just met her the other night at youth group. She's really good." He still had his hand on Krystal's, who glared at Mackenzie.

Mackenzie wished Bryce could see Krystal's face, but he was busy talking about the girl who was performing. "She goes to our school too, I think," Bryce continued. "I'm hoping she'll join the youth band."

"Do you play?" Mackenzie asked in her sweetest voice to annoy Krystal.

"I play bass guitar and drums." His attention was diverted to another girl who walked in the door. "Hey, it's Munchkin." He stood up and waved to a tiny girl with long blond locks and a giant smile almost bigger than she was.

Mackenzie looked at Krystal who rolled her eyes. *Hmm, another girl she doesn't like.*

The girl waved to Bryce, then stopped and pointed to the girl playing and singing at the front of the room. Bryce nodded his head and smiled.

"Hey Bryce! Hey K!" The tiny girl was practically bubbling over.

Bryce greeted her with a hug, then turned to Mackenzie. "This is our friend, Sadie," he said. "Affectionately known as Munchkin." He elbowed her in the ribs. "Sadie, this is Mackenzie and her brother, Trey. They're new to the school. She's a friend of Krystal's from the track team."

Mackenzie looked at Krystal whose mouth was a straight line across her face.

Bryce didn't seem to notice.

Sadie's bright blue eyes gleamed. "Oh, great to meet you guys." Her attention turned back to Bryce. "Did you meet Tammi at youth group last night?" She nodded her head at the singer.

"Uh, yeah." Bryce said. "You invited her but then left her all alone, Squirt." He pulled another chair to the table.

Sadie plopped down. "Well, Lauren actually did the inviting," she said. "She's so good. Wouldn't it be great to have her in the youth band?"

Krystal scooted her chair away from Sadie's a bit. "Why don't we actually listen to this amazingly talented girl?" She snarled.

Sadie giggled, nudging her shoulder into Krystal's. "You always make me laugh."

"Let's get going," Mackenzie whispered to Trey.

Trey stood and Mackenzie followed his lead while Sadie now moved into her seat. She moved behind Bryce, leaned down and whispered in his ear. "We gotta go. Can you get me my book?"

Before Bryce could respond, Krystal was on the other side of him, keys in hand. "I'll go. You listen to the music." She rubbed Bryce's shoulder. "Let's go," she said, turning her back to Mackenzie.

They followed Krystal through the maze of tables to the front door. Mackenzie tried to holler for her to slow down but Krystal either didn't hear because of the music or she was ignoring her. Most likely it was the latter.

When they got outside, Krystal faced them, her expression resembling a drill sergeant. "My car's over there. I'll go grab your book and bring it to you."

She came back with the book in hand. "One math book," she said, shoving it into Mackenzie's hand.

"Thanks," Mackenzie said. "And don't forget what we talked about today."

Krystal's face tightened. She glanced in Trey's direction and back to Mackenzie. "Right. See you at practice."

Trey watched Krystal reenter the noisy coffee shop. "What's with her?"

Mackenzie laughed in hopes of playing off her fear. "Aw, she's just ticked because I beat her record for the 800-meter."

"Mm-hmm, so you beat her record *and* you're trying to steal her boyfriend?"

Mackenzie gave Trey a shove. "Let's go."

Chapter 18

TAMMI held the last note on her guitar, opening her eyes to the applause—whoops and cheers from the back of the room. She leaned forward on her stool and squinted, spotting Sadie and Bible Study Boy from last night.

You gotta be kiddin' me.

Taking in a deep breath and closing her eyes again, she began finger-picking her guitar. Soon she was lost in her music, on a journey that transported her to heights only known when she played. This was where she felt most comfortable, most like herself. There was a love-hate relationship with performing, torn between sharing her music with others, in hopes they could become part of the rapture, and despising the stares of an audience.

Once finished, she slid from the stool and made a beeline toward the front door. She opened it before realizing she'd left her guitar case inside. *Dang it!* She didn't want to go back in but was now forced to.

Through the glass doors, she could see Sadie and the Bible study guy heading in her direction. She mumbled a curse word, then leaned her shoulder into the door to open it, the smell of freshly brewed coffee smacking her in the face.

"Oh, good! You're coming back." Sadie approached with her arms extended as if she wanted to hug her.

Tammi swerved to one side, avoiding the possible embrace. "Uh, yeah, I need my case."

The Bible study guy smirked at her lack of enthusiasm toward Sadie's affection. "So we meet again," he said. "That was amazing music, by the way."

Sadie grabbed hold of Tammi's wrist. "Come and sit with us," she said, pulling slightly.

"W-wait. I need to grab my case."

"Oh, Bryce can get it for you." Sadie chirped.

Bryce. That's his name.

Tammi pulled free. "I'll get it and meet you over at your table."

Ugh, what am I doing?

She contemplated bolting out the door before they noticed, then remembered Sadie's terrified expression from last night. She hated when her compassion overrode her common sense.

Sadie seemed her overly cheerful self now. But there was no mistake about what she'd seen. It bore deep into her soul. Sadie had a past similar to hers. Underneath all the friendliness, was a scared and broken girl, just like herself.

When Tammi approached their circular table, Sadie moved over, politely opening a seat between herself and Bryce. Tammi noticed a popular girl from school named Krystal sitting on the other side of Bryce. Krystal had her elbow on the table, her face resting on her fist.

"So you've met Bryce," Sadie said. "This is Krystal."

Tammi sat down. "Hi, I'm Tammi."

Krystal didn't budge. "It's an honor." Her voice was monotone.

Bryce nudged Krystal's elbow causing her chin to slip from her fist. Krystal glared at Bryce, then a sliver of a smile threatened to crack her stone-like features when he puckered his lips giving her an air kiss.

Sadie laughed. "We're such a loving bunch!"

"Speak for yourself," Krystal said.

Tammi found herself chuckling. She might actually like this Krystal girl.

Bryce shook his head. "That's my cynical Krystal."

"More like *real*," she fired back. "All those Bible studies have made you—"

Bryce gently placed his index finger on Krystal's lips. "Shh, we don't need to go *there*."

Tammi felt like she was watching a tennis match. Her head turned from Bryce, to Sadie to Krystal. She was surprisingly entertained.

"You left last night before we had band practice," Bryce said. "I hope you'll come back. I think you'd like it. Plus, I'm dying to accompany you."

Krystal grunted. "Seriously? Look at her. Does she seem like someone who wants to play in a dorky church band? I mean, she's actually *good*."

Tammi raised her pierced eyebrow then looked at Bryce. She noticed the muscles in his jaw twitch and tighten.

"You've never even heard us play," he said. "Not that I haven't invited you."

Sadie piped in. "Tammi heard the band at church on Sunday," she said, looking at Tammi. "Did you think it was dorky?"

"*You* go to church?" Krystal asked, looking from Tammi's feet back to her face again.

Tammi looked down at what she was wearing: a pair of black and white high top Chucks, some cut-off denim shorts with ripped black fishnet hose beneath showing the tattoo on her upper thigh. The ensemble was complete with a Rolling Stones tee shirt she'd cut the neck out of so it hung off one shoulder, drawing attention to a butterfly tattoo. "Yeah, *I* go to church."

Sadie's face lit up like she'd just spotted Santa Claus, and Bryce crossed his arms, nodding his head and smiling smugly.

Krystal, on the other hand, laughed. "Oh, come on." She leaned forward to look at Tammi.

Tammi shrugged. "What can I say, the church band is rockin'." She leaned back in her chair. "I'll admit I'm not so sure about the lyrics, but the band's good."

Krystal laughed. "Uh-huh, that's what I thought. And did *he* invite you to go?" She motioned to Bryce.

Before Tammi could answer, he said, "The youth band is really good too."

Tammi didn't like where this was leading. She only wanted to put Krystal in her place, not get roped into more church. "So I gotta bail." She rose from her seat.

Bryce started to get up. "I'll walk you out." His green eyes sparkled.

Tammi looked down at Bryce, placed her hand on his shoulder, gently pushing him back in his seat. "I'm capable of walking out all by myself, Church Boy."

Krystal and Sadie erupted into harmonious laughter. "Burn!" They cheered.

Bryce took it in stride, leaning his head back and played like he was trying to pull a dagger out of his chest.

Tammi shook her head. "I'm so onto your little church boy act," she smirked, pulling her guitar case over her shoulder. "See ya." She patted his cheek.

Sadie and Krystal's hyena laughter rang out as she strolled away. "Now, I like *that* church girl." Krystal said.

She smirked. *Church girl—ha! Never been called that before.*

Outside, Tammi turned to see Sadie back inside, waving goodbye to Krystal and Bryce and about to head in her direction. *Oh, no!*

Sadie stopped and refilled her drink.

Tammi hurried to her car before Sadie could catch up. She opened the door, tossed her guitar in the back seat, and smiled as the engine started. Catching a glimpse of Sadie's blonde hair, she pulled out of the parking lot. *Whew!*

Strange, but in a way she felt like she'd hung out with friends. She'd never really had many friends. And since moving in with her grandparents, she pretty much stayed to herself. Oh, but there were always the familiar gawks and ogling from guys. Unsolicited attention that made her skin crawl when they undressed her with their eyes. After the mistakes with her last boyfriends, she vowed not to go down that road ever again.

Noticing the market ahead, Tammi suddenly remembered Grandma had asked her to bring home milk. She jerked the wheel to the right, nearly missing the entrance to the parking lot. She hurried in and bought the milk. When she came back outside the sky had darkened and was beginning to sprinkle. She ran to her car as the sprinkles turned to heavy rain.

Climbing in, Tammi leaned forward and folded her arms across the steering wheel contently listening to the rhythm of the raindrops. She thought about Bryce.

Even though he was a flirt, he didn't look at her the way other guys did. He was kind and polite. A good Christian guy that her grandparents would love. Probably a virgin too.

She breathed in deeply, letting out a sigh. They were opposites— him pure and her damaged beyond repair. What would Bryce, or anyone, for that matter, think if he knew she'd had sex with her own father?

She shuddered, feeling a chill run up her spine. Incest had joined her and was caressing the back of her neck with one bony-clawed finger. Tammi sat back in her seat and started the engine. She shuddered again and pulled onto the highway.

The rain was now coming down in sheets, smearing across the windshield. She fumbled around unsuccessfully trying to locate the knob for the wipers when she saw headlights flying directly toward her. Panic surged from her toes to the top of her head like an electrical shock. The headlights came fast. Then there was the crunching sound of metal and glass. She felt her body snap. And all went black.

Chapter 19

SADIE attempted to raise her hand in front of her face to block the bright light, but pain surged up her arm preventing her from lifting it. She winced, feeling as though tiny shards of glass were stabbing every inch of her body.

She heard a muffled voice in the distance. "Can you hear me, darlin'? What's your name?"

Her body was being lifted. Eyes squeezed shut, she opened her mouth to cry out but pain stole her breath. Nearby voices sounded like they were under water.

"Did you get this one's name?" A man's voice asked.

"No. The girl in the other car is about the same age and unconscious."

Sadie heard the distant cry of a siren, which instantly jarred a terrifying recollection of what happened. A scream blurted out of her mouth.

"We're gonna take care of you. Hang in there," a kind male voice said.

The sirens wailed closer and closer, then came to a halt. Someone touched her leg. A million knives sent shockwaves of pain to the bone. Gritting her teeth, she tried to open her eyes, but the pain was unbearable. The voices and sounds grew faint. She felt lighter, like she was floating and fading away.

The room was sterile and white. Looking down, Sadie saw a team of doctors and nurses performing a surgery. She tilted her head for a better look at the patient, when she caught sight of an enormous angelic being standing to her right. Brilliant beams of light shone all around him. His eyes burned like clear-blue torches. His face was a cross between a man and a lion. He had massive wings that towered above his head, and he was moving in her direction. With his muscular arm, he motioned for Sadie to look again at the patient. She caught a glimpse of long blond hair. Her eyes darted back to the angel. He was still pointing to the table. She looked again and gasped. It was *her* broken body lying on the table!

"NO!" she cried. "I'm not ready. Oh, please, I'm not ready!"

The angel took hold of Sadie in his stalwart arms. She leaned over, looking at her body below as they rose into a blinding beam of light. Sadie heard the most beautiful music she'd ever heard but could still hear the voices of the nurses. A graceful figure of a woman wearing a shimmering gown was approaching with her arms held out to embrace Sadie—her real mama!

"Her pulse is dropping."

She turned her head toward the operating team. Her back arched, then relaxed.

"Stay with us, Sadie," a doctor said.

There was the sensation of spinning and falling simultaneously. Then with a jolt, she was lying on the table choking for air, back inside her own body again.

"We've got her!" A voice said.

Sadie's eyes fluttered open. She was instantly dragged into a rippling wave of excruciating pain all over her body. Although her vision was fuzzy, she saw someone dressed in white moving closer to her.

"Well, look who's awake," a familiar voice said. It was her adopted mother. "Oh, thank God!"

"What happened?" Sadie croaked. Surprised by the sound that came out of her, she tried to lift her hand to her throat, but the pain wouldn't allow her to.

Her mother's gentle voice spoke close in her ear. "Oh, sweetie, don't try to move. You were in a car accident, but you're going to be okay."

"Ooh," Sadie winced. "It was raining really hard." She paused to take a labored breath. "I dropped my coffee, and then—oh, gosh!" Sadie began to weep.

Her mother touched her forehead. "Sadie, it's okay, sweetie."

Sadie heaved and coughed. "There was a car," she managed. "On the wrong side of the road! The other car—are they all right?"

When her mother didn't answer, she began rolling her head back and forth, tears streaming down her pale cheeks. "Mom, did I kill someone?" She strained to focus on her mother's face.

Her mom placed her hand on Sadie's face to stop her from moving. "The other driver was a student like you. She's in a coma. The doctors are hopeful she'll wake soon though," she said calmly.

Sadie screamed and thrashed more violently.

"I'm going to increase her pain medication. This should help calm her too," a nurse said.

Instant relief warmed her veins throughout her body. It was as though she was slipping into a dream, and yet she could still hear her mother speaking. Or was it praying? It was hard to tell.

Chapter 20

KRYSTAL pulled into Bryce's rosebush-lined driveway on the way to school Tuesday morning. His broken-down Mustang at the side of the garage didn't match with the perfectly manicured home. Bryce's dad seemed to always be outside working on something. She twisted her bottom lip thinking about the rundown condition of hers since dad had left. When Bryce didn't immediately show up, she tooted the horn.

He rounded the corner talking on his cell phone.

Ugh! It better not be that weasel Mackenzie!

He waved to Krystal and continued the phone call as he entered the car. "No, I'm glad you called, Kenzie," he said in a soft, almost whisper voice. "I'll tell Krystal right now." He took in a deep breath. "Okay, I'll see ya at school. Bye."

So, it's 'Kenzie' now. How sickening.

Bryce stuffed the phone in his pocket then stared down at his lap.

Krystal gripped the steering wheel tightly, ready for him to admonish her for bullying poor little *Kenzie* whose mom is in the hospital.

"There was a car accident last night." His voice was somber.

"Who?"

He looked at her square in the face. "Munchkin and Tammi, the singer. It must have happened when they were driving home from the Grind."

Krystal gasped. "How bad?"

Bryce raked his fingers through his hair. "Tammi's in a coma. Sadie's conscious. Sounds pretty bad."

Krystal released her grip from the steering wheel and sat back in the seat. "Wow." She puffed out a deep breath of air, making a hissing sound. "Hey, wait," she said. "How does Mackenzie know about the accident?"

"They're at the same hospital as her mom. I guess her dad told her." Bryce pulled out his phone. "I better text my mom. She'd want to know so the church can put them on the prayer chain."

"The what? Are you kidding me right now?"

He rolled his eyes then continued to text. "Maybe we can go over to the hospital after practice?" He was looking at her again.

Krystal glanced from the road to Bryce. "Well, I don't know. I mean, they probably only want family right now."

He nodded. "Yeah, I bet you're right." Bryce looked at his phone. "My mom said our pastor already knows about it and is going to the hospital."

"I guess they'll let a pastor in," Krystal said.

"My mom said Tammi's grandparents have been going to the church for years. It's kinda weird we just barely met."

He looked out the window. "I can't believe this. It's so strange. We just saw them both like twelve hours ago." He looked at Krystal now. "I think this is what Pastor Dave was preaching about. You never know when your last day is. We act as though we'll live forever."

She twisted her neck to look at him. "Sheesh. No one's dead." She looked back to the road.

"It's just, we take life for granted, ya know? It's like we don't think bad things can happen to us or people we know."

"Maybe in your perfect world. Look around you, Bry. Life's crappy."

KRYSTAL was relieved when classes were over. She couldn't wait to get out on the track and run. Instead, on her way to the gym she ran into Mackenzie.

"Bryce told you about the accident?" she asked Krystal as if they were old friends.

So much nerve!

"Yeah, it's pretty weird. Do you know how it happened?" Krystal played along like they *were* friends—for now.

"My dad says it may've been because of the rain. It was pouring."

Krystal found herself examining Mackenzie's profile as they walked. Her pale skin was flawless except for the little freckles across her narrow nose. "Uh, do you know much about their injuries?" She asked.

"Not any more than I told Bryce," Mackenzie didn't look at Krystal. "I'm looking forward to running on the track."

Krystal nodded. "Yeah, I was thinking the same thing. Sometimes it's the only thing that feels right."

Mackenzie turned to her. "I know, right?"

Well, we do have something in common.

Bailey, Alexis, and some of the others from track were gathered outside of the gym. Bailey's rabbit-toothed grin met them—both of them. Krystal's eyes narrowed as she realized the team had accepted Mackenzie and now they thought *she* did as well.

Mackenzie smiled thinly, looking down while she kept walking to the doors.

"Hey, are you two like BFFs now?" Bailey asked with a giggle.

Mackenzie glanced over her shoulder and chuckled but didn't stop walking. Bailey playfully shoved her shoulder into Krystal's.

"Hee-hee."

Krystal rolled her eyes and entered the locker room.

She walked past Mackenzie, who was already changing into her shorts. Her legs were long and skinny but also muscular.

Mackenzie looked up, briefly making eye contact.

Once at her locker, Krystal kept sneaking peeks at Mackenzie. She slid off her jeans and looked down at her own legs. Both of Mackenzie's legs would make one of hers. At least she had some color though. Mackenzie was a ghost with pointy elbows and knobby knees. Who was she kidding? She'd love to be skinny.

Mackenzie walked by, pulling her hair into a pony tail and pulling Krystal from her thoughts. "See ya out there."

I guess I'll keep playing along. Keep your friends close and your enemies closer.

Right on cue, Anger inched up behind Krystal, placing its clawed fingers on her shoulders, spouting vicious lies into her ear. Its smaller, shriveled head grew larger and larger and began speaking at the same time as the other grotesque head. Their low voices growled chaotically like two radio stations playing at the same time, but in different languages. Finally, they converged, speaking in one voice. "There will be no friendship. Mackenzie is a divisive witch!"

Krystal hurried to tie her shoes so she could catch up to Mackenzie before the other girls came out. She jogged up next to her. "Is your mom still in the hospital?"

Mackenzie's dark brows scrunched, making vertical lines between them. "Uh, yeah," she answered. "Why?"

"I guess I was thinking that maybe you could check on that Tammi girl and Sadie if you go to see her."

Krystal knew she'd hit a nerve. She looked out at the track casually, but could see Mackenzie looking at her from her peripheral vision.

"I haven't really seen my mom since that day you and Bryce saw me at the hospital." Mackenzie said. "Maybe you and Bryce could go. I mean, I don't really know them."

"Oh." Krystal wished she hadn't asked, hearing the pain in Mackenzie's voice.

Mackenzie was quiet for a few seconds, then turned to look at her. "My dad is the one who told me about the whole thing. He goes to see my mom every day. I can ask him to find out more."

"Okay, whatever." Krystal huffed. "So I guess we should go do our stretches." She walked a few paces in front of Mackenzie to let her know the conversation was done.

As Krystal did her warm ups and drills, her thoughts turned to Mackenzie's mom. What was the deal with that? Why hadn't Mackenzie been to see her? Something was strange about it. She thought about her own mom who was probably drinking to mask her depression since her dad left. Then it hit Krystal. Mackenzie's mom tried to commit suicide! That *had* to be it. For some reason, she just *knew*.

A knot formed in Krystal's stomach. She glanced around the track. She spotted Mackenzie from a distance, running hard and fast. Her thick, black ponytail flew behind her while her legs pumped mechanically like a locomotive. Krystal was torn between jealousy and pity. Mackenzie was a bullet, and that was irksome. But she also recognized that get-out-all-of-the-pain-and-anger-and-run-for-your-life mentality. She'd been doing it herself for months. In fact, it had made her stronger and faster.

Coach blew the whistle, signaling the team for a meeting near the bleachers. But Mackenzie just kept running.

"I'll get her, Coach," Krystal said, jogging out to Mackenzie on the track. When Krystal was just behind her, Mackenzie quickly turned her head over her shoulder, then began running at breakneck speed.

The competition was on! Any ounce of pity Krystal may have felt earlier was obliterated—with a little help from Anger. Fueled by emotion, she flew past Mackenzie like she had wings. She heard her gravelly footsteps nearly on top of her. Throwing back her head and chest, Krystal pushed herself to go faster. All the while, Anger's two voices spoke in unison. "Win! Win!"

She could hear her teammates cheering and Coach blowing the whistle as she reached the orange cones, Mackenzie right on her heels and then beside her.

Both girls were neck and neck when Krystal felt Mackenzie's leg brush against her own. The next thing she knew, they'd become an entanglement of arms and legs, colliding to the dirt in a painful thud.

Chapter 21

MACKENZIE bit the side of her mouth when she landed face first into the chalky, brown dirt. She rolled onto her side to see Krystal curled in a fetal position, her back to Mackenzie.

Coach stood over the two of them. "What were you guys thinking? Krystal?" She bent down to touch her. "Where's the pain?"

Krystal flopped over like a fish. "HER! She's the pain!" She twisted her body closer to Mackenzie's.

Mackenzie put her hand up to block Krystal, who was now clawing at her hair, but instead she accidentally whacked Krystal in the face. Krystal's eyes were black slits when she lunged on top of Mackenzie.

Pushed into survival mode, Mackenzie balled her hands into fists and hammered them into Krystal's face. Pain seethed from her scalp as Krystal pulled out a clump of her hair. She smelled Krystal's sweat as the two of them rolled, punched, and scratched like animals.

Coach Lopez pulled Krystal off Mackenzie. "Enough!" Coach hollered. "In my office. Both of you."

Mackenzie wobbled to her feet, noticing the entire track team, as well as the boys' track and baseball teams had become an audience to their knock-down drag-out brawl. She dusted her shirt, wiped the hair from her face, and followed behind Krystal, who appeared to be limping. She felt someone's eyes on her. There was Bryce in the distance, shaking his head with arms folded across his chest. Mackenzie pursed her lips and looked away.

When she got to Coach's office, Krystal was already sitting down. Coach stood behind her desk and glared at both girls.

"Mackenzie, wait outside." She sighed. "Don't go far. And shut the door."

Mackenzie sat on a bench just outside the office with her hands in her lap. Oh, how she wanted to go to the bathroom and clean up, but Coach said not to go far. She had to pee and could feel the blood, gravel, and dirt crusted on her knees and elbows. The rest of the team approached the gym's double doors in a commotion. Some were laughing. She kept her head down while the girls filed inside. Mackenzie recognized Bailey's shoes standing directly in front of her. Bailey handed her a wet wipe. Mackenzie took it, lifting her chin to see Bailey's droopy mouth.

"Krystal's a bully," she said before walking away.

After several minutes, the office door opened. Mackenzie looked up to see Coach peering down at her. "Okay, your turn." She waved Mackenzie in.

Mackenzie waited until Krystal exited and was just out of reach before she went in.

"Krystal, have a seat on the bench," Coach said.

Krystal's shoulders slumped as she turned back around to sit on the bench. Coach closed the door. "Sit." She pointed to the chair in front of her desk.

Mackenzie brushed her long bangs from her eyes and sat, placing one hand on top of the other to keep from shaking.

Coach Lopez dragged her chair next to hers. "Look, Mackenzie, you're not in trouble here."

Mackenzie sighed. Her lower lip quivered. "I—I don't know what happened."

Coach leaned over, tilting her head to look at Mackenzie who was staring at her lap. "I know what happened," she said softly. "Why don't you tell me about the first time Krystal got physical with you?"

Closing her eyes, Mackenzie hoped to block the tears she felt welling up. "I'd rather not," she whispered.

"We're going to get to the bottom of this," Coach said. "Krystal tells me your mom is in the hospital."

Mackenzie opened her eyes, turning to Coach. "That doesn't have anything to do with this."

"Actually it does," Coach responded. "I care about my team. I care about you, Mackenzie, and I care about Krystal. Both of you have some extenuating circumstances I think have fueled some extreme emotions. We need to channel those emotions into running."

"That's what I was *trying* to do," Mackenzie said.

Coach nodded. "Yes, but when you saw Krystal run up alongside, you challenged her to a competition. I know you didn't use words to do this, but you challenged her nonetheless."

Mackenzie nodded her head in agreement. "Yes, but—"

Coach interrupted. "I know you didn't intend for a fight to break out. You were defending yourself. I saw the whole thing go down," she said. "Listen, I'm going to have Krystal come back in. Then the three of us are going to work on behaving like a team. But for now, I want you to know I will be calling your father to let him know what happened as well as Krystal's mom."

"Okay."

Coach Lopez brought Krystal back, and spoke to the girls on what being a team means. She gave Krystal a warning that another incident of bullying would result in dismissal from team.

"Okay," Coach said walking toward the door. "I'm going to be right outside. I want the two of you to talk and work things out. When I come back in, I want you both to tell me a few things you talked about."

The door opened, letting in the sounds of the noisy locker room, then quickly closed to complete silence. Mackenzie could hear Krystal breathing. She didn't want to look at her.

Finally, Krystal spoke up. "Did you tell her my secret?"

Mackenzie frowned. She didn't know what Krystal was talking about. She sat quietly racking her brain when Krystal spoke again. "No one knew until today. Coach told me she had the same problem in high school. Now she's going to tell my mom, so I can get *help*."

Suddenly Mackenzie knew. *She thinks I told Coach that she's bulimic.* Then she realized Krystal must have told Coach first.

"I guess I'm just a mean, screwed-up person," Krystal said. "I'm sorry."

Mackenzie sat still, except for her legs that wouldn't stop bouncing. A million thoughts were running through her head.

"Are you going to say anything?" Krystal broke her thoughts.

Mackenzie took in a deep breath. "Well, first of all, I did *not* tell Coach anything about the day we met in the bathroom. I didn't tell her about any of your bullying either. And secondly, what are you actually sorry for?" Mackenzie asked. "What I mean is, are you just sorry it's all come out? Or are you sorry that you bullied and hurt me?"

Krystal's cheeks puffed as she let out a long burst of air. "Sheesh, hardcore," she said. "To be honest, it's a bit of both. Probably more the first one. But, you aren't completely innocent here either."

Mackenzie felt heat rising in her face. *She has so much nerve!*

"Okay, what are talking about?" Mackenzie asked, shifting her body toward Krystal, noticing the scratches she'd put on Krystal's face. "Is it that you think I'm after Bryce? Yeah, he's totally cute and nice and a *flirt*. But I'm not after him. And as far as beating your stupid record goes, oh, well! I'm not going to hold back for you. I'm a great runner, and I need to get a scholarship."

Krystal raised her eyebrows. Mackenzie wasn't sure if she should back away or duck. But Krystal just sat quietly.

"Are *you* going to say anything?" Mackenzie asked this time.

"You *knew*." Krystal spoke in almost a whisper, looking down at her feet. "You knew about my secret, and you still said those things about being thinner and faster than me." She looked at Mackenzie, with watery eyes. "And I'm pretty sure your mom tried to commit suicide, but you still did those mean things to me."

Mackenzie's shoulders dropped. A pang hit her in the gut like a sucker punch. She tried to draw in a breath, but air came in staggered wisps while heaving uncontrollably. Then the tears started. *Dang it!* There was nowhere to go. Nowhere to hide. She sat defenseless, drawing her knees up in the chair and sobbing into them. Oh, if only she could just disappear!

The door opened and Coach came in. *This just keeps getting better!*

Mackenzie's head whipped up and her legs went down in one fluid motion. She wiped the snot from her nose with the back of her hand and stared at the tiles on the floor. She didn't want Coach to see she'd been crying. Plus, she was sick of the drama herself. Time to pull it together.

Coach was like a dog who'd sunk her teeth into a bone and wasn't letting go. She droned on about team spirit and sisterhood for another ten minutes, then finally released them.

Once they shut the door to Coach's office, Krystal looked at Mackenzie. "For whatever it's worth, I really *am* sorry."

Mackenzie swept a stray piece of hair from her face. "It's worth a lot if you really mean it. Do you?"

"Yeah. You think I'd just say it?"

Mackenzie chewed on her lip. "That's true. You're too proud for that," she said. "Listen, I'm sorry, too. But I didn't say anything to Coach about your secret and wasn't planning on it either."

"I know. Thanks," Krystal looked down like she was embarrassed.

"Ya know, maybe it will be okay. I mean, it's not good to do that to yourself. You need to get some help," Mackenzie said. Krystal jerked her head up, her mouth a straight line. "Hey, I know it's not my place to say. Sorry."

"You're probably right. I just don't want to talk to my mom," Krystal said. "She'll be calling her psychologist friends and crap like that when she's got her own problems to deal with."

Mackenzie shook her head. "You were right about my mom. That's all I want to say about that though," she said. "I gotta get home, but I hope things can be better with us." She turned and headed toward her locker.

"Wait," Krystal said. "Did you mean what you said about Bryce? I mean, not being interested in him?"

Mackenzie thought of Bryce's gorgeous face. "Look, I'm not saying I don't think he's a totally cute and great guy, but I'm not trying to make him like me, if that's what you mean."

"Whatever. Fair enough, I guess," Krystal said. Their shoulders brushed as she walked past Mackenzie.

Mackenzie rolled her eyes. *She's so darned difficult!*

Chapter 22

TAMMI'S body lay motionless on the hospital bed. She looked like a mummy with her head and neck covered with bandages. Her long black hair pushed out of the top of the bandages like a rooster's crest. The blinds were drawn closed. A heart monitor beeped rhythmically while a ventilator whooshed. Beep, beep. Whoosh. Beep, beep. Whoosh.

Her grandparents slept in chairs—Grandpa in the corner, and Grandma leaning her slight frame over the bed.

The door opened and a pale, ragged-looking man slipped in and stood near Tammi's bed. His mostly gray hair hung in matted strings near his shoulders, one strand sticking to his unkempt, salt-and-pepper beard. His clothes were threadbare and dirty.

The man reached out a trembling hand. "Oh, my beautiful girl."

Tammi's grandma woke with a start, sitting up straight. She caught sight of him and stood to her feet. "Stan," her voice quivered as she called Tammi's grandpa.

Grandpa opened his eyes and gasped. "Mitch? Is that you?" He walked toward him.

Tears streamed into his scraggly beard. "Yes, Dad," he rasped in a voice that sounded older than Grandpa's.

Grandpa walked toward him with his arms open.

Mitch backed away, shaking his head. "I don't deserve that." He continued to shuffle backward toward the door.

A nurse walked in, and Tammi's dad backed up against the wall. He slowly slid down to the floor, holding his hands to his head moaning, "I'm sorry. I'm so sorry."

The nurse walked out quickly, calling for assistance. Another nurse came in and led him out of the room.

"I don't need help," her father said from outside the door. "I'm beyond help."

Grandma started to follow the nurse when she heard Tammi whimper and dashed back to the bed. "Tammi, honey," her voice croaked.

Grandpa came near, placing his hand gently on Tammi's bandaged hand. "Tammi, your grandma and I are right here. Please wake up."

Tammi's eyes fluttered and slowly opened. She managed a moan through the mask on her face.

"Oh, praise God!" Her grandma whispered.

Tammi squinted. She tried to move her arms, but they were restrained to keep her from pulling at the various tubes and IV.

"Tammi, there was a terrible accident. You're going to be okay. You're in the hospital. Do you remember?" Grandpa asked.

Grandma opened the door and hollered for a nurse. A nurse rushed to check the machines. The door opened again. A young doctor came in, looking down at a clipboard and notes. His head jerked up sharply when he realized what was occurring. "Oh, good. She's coming to. Okay, folks. You'll need to step out for a bit."

Grandpa put his arm around Grandma. They walked to a bench outside of Tammi's room and sat down.

"Well, at least she's awake," Grandpa said.

Grandma leaned her head against his shoulders. "I wonder where they took Mitch." Her watery eyes scanned the hall.

Grandpa kissed her head. "Stay here. I'm going to find out." He headed for the nurse's station.

Grandma watched him talking to a nurse. She strained to hear, but couldn't make out the conversation. A nurse nodded and touched her husband's shoulder, then he was on his way back to her.

Grandpa raked his hands through his sparse white hair. "He refused to be seen. The nurse said it appeared he's been living on the streets," he said. "I'll see to that later, my dear. Pastor knows folks at the homeless shelter. Maybe they've seen Mitch. But right now, we must stay here for Tammi." He sat next to his wife, taking her hand in his.

Grandma scowled, a tear sliding down her cheek. "I'm sick to my stomach thinking of what he put that poor child through."

Grandpa put his arm around his wife's thin shoulders. The two sat, huddled in each other's arms. With their heads bowed, each took a turn softly praying. Silas stoically stood guard over them, joining them in prayer. He lifted his strong arms heavenward. The prayers swirled in a pale blue cloud above their heads and rose through the ceiling. A gaggle of demons perched outside of Tammi's window caught sight of the iridescent cloud. They shrieked, their gangly bodies sailing in all different directions, abandoning their post.

The doctor approached and waited with his head bowed as though he sensed something sacred. After a moment, he cleared his throat. "You can see her now." His eyes sparkled with hope.

The room was transformed. Warm sunlight streamed in through the open blinds glistening over Tammi's bed. She was now fully awake, wide-eyed, looking in their direction. The ventilator had been removed from her mouth.

When Tammi parted her lips to speak, nothing came out. She scrunched her eyes in frustration.

The doctor spoke up. "As you can see, Tammi is alert, but is having trouble with speech. This is a result of the traumatic brain injury she incurred in the accident," he said. "We'll be running more tests in a while. The important thing is she's awake, understands what's being said, and is breathing on her own."

"Oh, Tammi, honey," Grandma said, her eyes filling with tears.

Grandpa put his arms around Grandma. "Praise God!"

Tammi squeezed her eyes shut, then opened her mouth again, trying to speak. This time a grunt came out. She strained to sit up but was too weak. Grandma touched Tammi's arm. "Honey, it's going to take some time. It's okay."

Tammi puckered her lips, but again only a gravelly grunting noise proceeded out. She closed her eyes and rolled her head furiously back and forth on her pillow.

"Tammi, this is most likely a temporary condition," the doctor said, then looked at Tammi's grandparents. "Let's go outside and talk. They'll be taking her for a CT scan and MRI shortly."

Grandma bent over Tammi's bed, her gray eyes looking directly into Tammi's. "We'll be back soon, honey," she said, stroking Tammi's cheek.

———

TAMMI watched the doctor and her grandparents walk away. The door closed with a thud. She felt a coldness come over her, bringing a familiar and unwanted feeling. Her insides twisted in fear. She recalled a dream of a homeless-looking man standing over her crying. Her teeth began to chatter and her body shook convulsively. Incest had crept back into the room, summoned by the scent of Tammi's fear.

Incest curled its scaled body around her head and whispered revolting things into her ear, spurring 3D images of her father's rough hands running up and down her legs. She could smell his beer breath and even hear his slurring words, "L-l-let Daddy help you f-f-feel better."

She shook her head, trying to break free from the torturous images her mind was playing like a horror movie. Somehow, in the background, she detected a lone voice—singing a song she recognized from her grandparents's church. A man's voice—full and robust—the most beautiful and soothing voice she'd ever heard. The song grew louder and louder, overpowering the unholy images, obliterating them with each note. Her body relaxed as though a warm blanket had been lovingly placed over her shoulders.

Silas stood next to Tammi's bed, his enormous wings touching the ceiling. He raised his hands above his head. As he sang, his glorious voice filled the room with a beautiful glow. Incest curled into a tight ball, transformed into a dark fog, then disappeared.

Tammi could swear the singing was right next to her. She opened her eyes and gasped. It *was* right next to her! The blinding light hid all but a giant silhouette, which vanished just as quickly.

What the heck was that?

Chapter 23

SADIE'S family, along with Grant and Lauren, huddled in the waiting room outside of the ICU Wednesday afternoon. They'd been told the good news Sadie was awake from the anesthesia and breathing on her own. The hospital strictly enforced their policy of only two visitors at a time, and Sadie's parents were already in the room. The others waited patiently for their turn to visit. Grant and Lauren held hands, leaning their heads together, while Sadie's younger brothers sat between their grandparents, playing a game on a cell phone.

SADIE was confused. She understood there had been an accident—her parents had explained last night when she'd regained consciousness. But she was groggy and in so much pain. She recalled a nurse giving her pain medication, and her mother kissing her cheek. Then she was in and out of sleep, dreaming she had died and gone to heaven. Now, this morning her parents stood before her, their faces bright with excitement. Sadie *had* to tell them.

"I think something happened to me after the accident," she said. Their smiles disappeared, but Sadie continued. "There was an angel. He was gigantic. He took me to heaven—" Her voice trailed off when she saw the perplexed looks on their faces.

Her mother sat on the bed next to Sadie. "Oh, sweetie," she said in a placating voice.

"I mean it. I'm serious," Sadie insisted. "I saw my body on the operating table. I saw nurses and doctors trying to fix me. I think it was my foot or leg. I was floating above my own body."

At that point a doctor came in and stood beside Sadie's bed. "Well, here's our little fighter," he said.

"It's *you*. You're the doctor I saw in the operating room." Sadie said.

The doctor scowled, squinting his beady brown eyes. "Yes, I am."

"I saw you. You were trying to fix my foot."

The doctor nodded slowly. "Y-yes—I *tried*," he said, pausing too long. "I'm sorry that I couldn't."

Sadie's spindly arms shook as she tried to push herself up to look at her feet. "What do you mean?" She kicked her legs beneath the blanket, causing her mother to jump off the bed.

"Take the blanket off, Mom."

Her mother's face was pale and her lower lip quivered. She looked at the doctor and then at Sadie's dad. The doctor came closer to Sadie, standing near her mother. His eyes squinted into tiny slits making them almost disappear. He ran his fingers through his neatly trimmed beard.

Sadie could tell she didn't want to hear what he had to say. She wanted to see for herself. "Take the blanket off!" she screamed.

The doctor stepped closer and pulled the blanket to one side, revealing a bandage that wrapped the bottom of her leg. Sadie swatted at the blanket, in effort to see her other leg. She glared down at her left leg and foot, then her eyes moved to the bandage on the other leg. She saw a rounded stump with a tube running from it. The tube stopped just before the place where her foot should be.

Sadie's arms began to shake, unable to hold her weight. She collapsed backward into the pillow. She heaved and coughed. "I was supposed ... to be in heaven with ... my real mama."

Sadie's mother turned her face away, stepping into her husband's arms. He stroked her hair and kissed the top of her head. There was a rap on the door as Pastor Dave entered. He looked at the doctor. "I'm the family pastor."

Sadie heard his voice and was filled with an inkling of hope. "Oh, Pastor Dave," she cried. "An angel took me to heaven."

He walked past the doctor, patting him on the back. He sat down on the bed near Sadie's bandaged leg.

She saw him quickly glance down and then back at her. Her heart shattered at the look on his face. "My foot," was all she could manage to say.

"I'm so sorry," Pastor Dave said, a tear trickling down his cheek. "I'm very relieved you came out of the accident alive."

"But I—there was this angel. He took me to heaven. I saw my real mama. Then I was back here in my body."

Pastor Dave's mouth turned upward, his blue eyes crinkled at the edges. "God still has work for you do to, Sadie. He knows how you miss your mama. I think he gave you the gift of seeing her to give you strength."

Sadie wiped her nose with the back of her trembling hand. "You really think so?"

"Well, I can't know for sure." He smiled again. "But I *do* know how much God loves us and gives us just what we need at just the right time."

Sadie's mom came closer to the bed. "I think you're right, Pastor Dave."

"You believe me?" Sadie asked.

Her father edged closer, hugging his wife from behind. They both nodded their heads.

The doctor spoke up. "This is not the first time I've heard of this kind of thing, Sadie," he said. "Not only do I believe you, but I'd like to spend some time later discussing what you saw. Right now, my main concern is your healing."

Sadie glanced down at her legs again. Her quick-lived excitement escaped like air from a deflating balloon. "How will I walk again?" Sadie asked. "Oh, my gosh!" She paused, drawing in a staggered breath. "How will I *dance*?"

Chapter 24

KRYSTAL looked at her reflection in the car visor's mirror. Even with heavy foundation, the yellow and green bruise under her eye stood out. She was sore and too embarrassed to see anyone, so eating lunch alone in her car was the plan. Tuesday, and everything that happened at track practice, replayed in her mind. Surprisingly, her mom didn't say a word at dinner last night. Maybe Coach didn't call her mom after all. Or maybe Mom was too much into her own issues. Even worse—maybe she was waiting for the *right* time to have a mother-daughter-heart-to-heart conversation. *Ugh!*

Krystal's phone vibrated, drawing her from her thoughts. Bryce. "Hello?"

"Where are you?"

She paused. "I just needed space. I'm in my car."

There was a tap on the passenger window. "Hey!" He laughed.

Krystal unlocked the door. "Why'd you call if you knew I was in my car?"

He opened the door and got in. "I'm just checking on you. I didn't want to startle you," he said, rubbing her arm with the back of his hand. "Are you okay? I mean after yesterday."

"I don't get you sometimes," she snapped. "You were quiet the whole way to school this morning. I thought you were mad at me for what happened with sweet little Mackenzie."

"Yeah, I know how you are in the mornings, K. I wasn't gonna bring up something like this until after noon, at least." He laughed again, shoving his shoulder into hers.

"So, you're not mad?" She didn't wait for an answer. "I attacked the poor new girl whose mom is in the hospital."

"One, I heard from Bailey that you and Mackenzie worked it out. Plus, I saw Mackenzie and we talked, too," he said.

"*Really*. What did Mackenzie tell you?"

Bryce cleared his throat. "Didn't say a whole lot. Probably embarrassed. And we just talked really quick before class. She just said that things were fine now." He paused. "Oh, she did say she sort of challenged you out on the track and got you angry."

Krystal was quiet. That was it? Mackenzie could've bad-mouthed her big time. But *didn't*. She looked at Bryce's handsome face. Why did he put up with her? "Yeah, I think Mackenzie and I realized it was stupid to be competing against each other. You were right, we do have stuff in common." She looked away for a moment, then back to him. "But she still kinda bugs me. She acts all innocent, but she's not."

Bryce laughed. "Everyone kinda bugs you, Krystal."

Krystal smiled. "True," she shrugged. "But that's because people are stupid."

"That's my Krystal," Bryce said, shaking his head. "Gotta love her."

Do you?

As Krystal approached the gym, there was Mackenzie talking with Bailey and some of the other girls from track. When Bailey caught sight of Krystal, her big toothy grin melted away like a snow cone in the summer. Mackenzie must have noticed too, because she turned around. "Hi," she said nonchalantly to Krystal.

Krystal fidgeted with the dangling strap from her backpack. "Hi," she said in her most smooth and in-control voice. "So, ya ready for another cat fight?" She chuckled and looked at Bailey, whose mouth was agape. "Oh my gosh, Bailey. Mackenzie and I are fine." Krystal rolled her eyes. "Right, Kenzie?"

Mackenzie's eyebrows rose. She hesitated while Krystal's insides quivered. "Yeah, we're good." Mackenzie finally said.

Krystal attempted to smile at Mackenzie, but her stupid lips trembled slightly. Flipping her long hair over her shoulder, she strolled past the group and into the gym.

Coach seemed to be eyeing Krystal and Mackenzie more than usual. When practice was over, she asked to see them both in her office.

Mackenzie sat quietly, staring down at her track shoes, the sides covered in red dirt.

Krystal considered saying something, but thought better. So instead, she busied her mind glancing around the room. A coat rack with a few jackets and umbrella. A file cabinet with pictures of loved ones on top. A large sign hung over the top of the door: "Give it your all or don't do it at all." Her gaze paused at the awards that hung symmetrically on the wall behind the desk, waiting for whatever Coach was about to dish out.

Coach sighed deeply. "It was a good practice. I hope you both are able to continue to treat each other with the respect a teammate deserves."

Mackenzie looked up. "It won't be a problem, Coach."

Coach nodded. "Good to hear," she said, then looked at Krystal.

Krystal clenched her jaw, grinding her teeth a bit. "No problem here *either*."

Coach tilted her head, raising her perfectly manicured eyebrows. "Okay then. That's what I want to hear. And it better be what I *see* as well," she said. "Understood?"

"What do you think?" Mackenzie asked Krystal, putting her on the spot.

"I think," Krystal said, clearing her voice, giving herself a chance to think, "that we're on the same team and need to act like it."

Coach stood up. "Okay, get going then."

Mackenzie walked out first. Krystal examined her slim muscular legs from behind. Mackenzie turned around and Krystal quickly looked up at her face, hoping she didn't notice she'd been staring. "Was that just an act for Coach?"

Krystal shrugged. "Kind of."

Mackenzie raised her thin fingers to massage her temple. "What does that mean?"

"It means that things are better, but I still don't trust you."

Mackenzie's dark eyes widened. "*You* don't trust *me*? You're the one ..."

Just then, Bailey and Alexis came back into the gym. "Hey, Krystal, do you want to go to the Grind?" Alexis hollered across the room.

Krystal looked at Mackenzie. "Want to?"

Mackenzie nodded her head yes and walked away without saying a word.

Krystal gave her best fake smile. "Okay, I guess we'll meet you guys there."

Once Alexis and Bailey left, Krystal walked over to Mackenzie, who was slipping on her shoes. "Are you gonna go? I mean I was trying to be nice since they didn't invite you."

Mackenzie grabbed her bag. "I already told them I'd go when they invited me *before* practice." She put on her backpack. "See ya over there."

Krystal was quiet for a second. "Well, I guess I'll see if *Bryce* needs a ride." She took out her phone and began texting him.

When Krystal looked up from her phone, Mackenzie was already halfway out. The big metal door closed, echoing in the empty gym.

Sheesh, what does Mackenzie expect—that we'll be best buddies now?

Bryce texted back. *Yep. C U at the car in 20.*

When Bryce and Krystal walked into the coffee shop, Mackenzie was already there and talking with Alexis and Bailey. Krystal noticed that Bryce saw her too. Her stomach twisted. *Does he like her?*

"Go get us a seat and I'll order," Bryce said. "You want your usual?"

"Yeah, thanks," Krystal said, digging in her bag for some money.

"I got it. You've been driving me everywhere." He grabbed hold of her hand that held a five-dollar bill and gently pushed it away. He gave her a quick sideways hug. His touch turned her insides to Jell-O.

"Thanks," she whispered, then turned away before she fainted. He smelled so *good*. She could breathe in that scent forever.

She noticed Mackenzie had been watching. Krystal smiled. Good. She pulled up two extra chairs to the already crowded table.

Bailey pushed a card across the table at her. "This is a card for Sadie. We're all signing it." She gushed.

Krystal looked at it then back at Bailey. "How are you getting it to her?"

Bailey's pointy shoulders rose up and down. "I don't know."

Krystal rolled her eyes. "Well, who bought the card?"

Bryce sat down and looked at the card. "Aw, cool," he said reading what people had written. "But we need to get one for Tammi too."

Krystal nodded. "Well, I'm trying to figure out who got this card and how we're getting it to Sadie."

Mackenzie pushed another card to Bryce. "Here's a card for the other girl," she said. "I was going to give the cards to my dad to take there tonight when he goes to see my mom."

Bryce smiled at Mackenzie. "Oh, yeah. That's a good idea," he said.

So, Mackenzie got the cards?

Bryce turned to Krystal. "Hey, I bet my mom will have more information on their status. Pastor Dave was going over there today. I'll let you know when we're allowed to go too."

"Great," Krystal smiled weakly. *Just great.*

Chapter 25

Mackenzie noticed Krystal's brows scrunch together when she realized where the cards came from. *Everything's a competition with her. Can't I just do something without her thinking I'm trying to get a 'one up' on her?*

"Sadie and Tammi are conscious now," Bryce announced, looking at a text on his phone. "They're both in ICU, so no visitors yet." The excitement was gone from his voice.

Even though he was a major flirt, Bryce was a good guy. Mackenzie saw the tenderness in his face as he spoke. By the blatant icy stare from across the table, Krystal was keenly aware that Mackenzie was looking at him. *Good grief!*

"I have an idea," Mackenzie said. "How about *you* just take the cards for Sadie and Tammi and give them to your mom. She can give the cards to your priest, since he will probably see them before any of us can."

"Priest?" Krystal rolled her eyes.

Bryce chuckled. "Oh, you mean Pastor Dave," he corrected kindly. "That's a good idea, Kenzie."

That's the second time he'd called her Kenzie. Only her family called her that. She just knew her chest was probably all red and splotchy. *Dang it!* Hopefully he didn't notice.

But Krystal must have. "No worries, *Kenzie*," she laughed. "I don't know the difference either." *Was Krystal actually being sympathetic or did she just want to seem like it to Bryce? Who knows about her?*

"I thought you went to church with him," Mackenzie asked Krystal.

Bryce smirked. "I've been inviting her forever."

"Yep, and he never accepts N-O as an answer," Krystal said.

"Someday she'll give into my charms." Bryce continued to stare at Krystal while brushing his hand against her cheek.

Krystal was the one blushing now.

And that's when it hit Mackenzie. They liked each other. But neither of them had admitted it to the other. "So, how long have you two known each other?"

Krystal turned but Bryce answered first.

"We've been close ever since preschool when our moms discovered we were neighbors." He playfully tugged on a strand of Krystal's long brown hair that draped over her bare suntanned shoulder. "Our families have even taken vacations together. Well, we used to." Bryce paused, looked down, and then quickly changed the subject. "Hey, I just thought of this. You're a neighbor too." He reached for a fist bump.

Mackenzie shook her head and reluctantly raised her fist to his, then rose from her seat. "I'll be right back." She held up her phone as if she had a call. She placed the phone to her ear and walked away, pretending to talk, and headed outside where she stood with her back against the wall. A light breeze blew her hair back, carrying with it the scent of freshly brewed coffee and vanilla. She drew in a deep breath, and the tightness in her stomach began to dissipate. That is until Krystal opened the glass doors.

"What are you doing?" Krystal asked.

"I came out here where it's quiet."

"Well, Mr. Knight-in-Shining-Armor was ready to come check on you, but I told him I would. Was that your plan?"

Mackenzie frowned. "For *you* to come and check on me? Of course not."

Krystal didn't seem amused with Mackenzie's witty comeback. "You didn't even have a call, did you?"

Mackenzie felt heat rising up her neck again.

Krystal eyes bulged. "Oh my gosh! You little—"

Mackenzie held up her hand. "Okay, I didn't have a call."

"I knew it!" Krystal said.

"No, but it's not what you think. I'm just not good in social settings."

Krystal scowled. "What the heck are you saying?"

Mackenzie huffed. "Look, I'm an introvert. It wears me out to try to ..." she took another deep breath, wiping her hand on her pant leg. "... to try to fit in and make intelligent conversation in a group setting. Especially with a cute guy and a girl who I don't know if she's gonna hit me or maybe be my friend or what."

Krystal seemed speechless by Mackenzie's candor.

Mackenzie couldn't believe she'd opened up about her social ineptness to someone as cunning as Krystal. But it was out there now. So, she took another risk. "When're you going to tell Bryce how you *really* feel about him?"

Krystal folded her arms across her chest and stepped back. "Like that's your business."

"Didn't say it was. Just wondering."

"So, how's your mom? *Just wondering*," Krystal snapped, taking a step closer.

Mackenzie fought the tears that were welling up. Then words seemed to spill out without a thought. "Well, I'm not sure, but I think they've stuck her in the psych ward. If they haven't yet, they should. She'll probably try to kill herself again, especially since this isn't her first attempt." Mackenzie spat out. "Is that what you wanted to hear?"

Krystal sucked in her lower lip, biting at it, then finally spoke. "I'm sorry."

Mackenzie's voice was flat. "Why?"

"Well, why did you ask me about my feelings for Bryce?"

Mackenzie shook her head. "It's not the same thing at all, Krystal. You hit below the belt."

"You're right."

"Here's another question for you," she said. "You're so worried that he might like me, but do you even notice the way he looks at you?" Feeling more in control, Mackenzie flipped a strand of hair from Krystal's face, then turned and walked back into the coffee shop, nearly running into Bryce.

"Hey, I was just coming out to check on you two," he said, glancing over Mackenzie's shoulder at Krystal.

"I'm fine. You should probably check on her though." Mackenzie nodded toward the door.

Bryce's eyes widened and he quickly made his way out to Krystal.

Mackenzie turned around just in time to see the two of them in an embrace. *I must be crazy!*

Chapter 26

TAMMI had been in the hospital for three days. She lay motionless, looking at the ceiling when the door opened slowly.

She squinted at the disheveled figure slowly edging in her direction. It was the homeless man in her dream. The peace that had previously enveloped her evaporated like morning mist.

She opened her mouth to scream, but nothing came out. The man shuffled closer. She tried to scream again, this time making a grunting noise. He stopped and stared at her with piercing blue eyes. "Don't be afraid. I promise I won't hurt you."

Tammi recognized that raspy voice—her *father*. She watched him edge closer and closer. Just like when she was a small girl. She was like a trapped animal. Tammi clutched the blanket tightly, her hand gliding over something hard—the nurse's call button. Her eyes were locked on his as she discreetly pushed.

"Mitch?" Grandpa's voice came from behind her father. She let out the breath she'd been holding.

"I just need to know she'll be okay. Then I'll leave," her father said, his eyes still locked on hers.

Tammi felt the gentle touch of her grandma's hand on her arm. She had been so focused on her dad that she didn't see her. "Honey, it's all right. We're here."

Tammi felt her body begin to relax. She looked into her grandma's sweet face, full of love and peace. She wanted to dive into that peace.

"Mitch, Tammi will be okay," her grandpa said, moving closer to his son. "The doctor said they'll be running a lot of tests, but her condition is most likely temporary. Where are you staying, son? Can we help you?"

Tammi's father moved closer to her bed. It was hard to tell it was him beneath all the hair and filth. He looked frail and much older. She wrinkled her nose when she caught a whiff of a pungent odor.

He winced and took a step back. "I know I'm a mess. I'm sorry," he blurted out. "But I need you to know—" his voice quivered— "I'm s-s-so sorry. Sorry for everything." He turned away.

"Wait, Mitch." Grandpa followed. "I want to help you."

Her father turned around and held up a shaky hand. "There's nothing for you to do. I deserve everything that's happened to me and more. I deserve to rot in hell."

"Oh, son." Her grandpa moved closer, grabbing her father's hand, holding it between both of his, ignoring the filth. "I forgive you. And God will forgive you too, if you'll ask."

"You don't know what I've done or you wouldn't say that."

"Jesus Christ died for your sins and mine, son."

Mitch pulled his hand away. "Your *worst* sin cannot compare to …" He inched closer in Tammi's direction, looked down at the floor and mumbled, "I hope you can find peace for yourself. I don't expect forgiveness. I'm a sick man." His voice became a whisper. "And the cancer will eat at my flesh like piranhas, and I deserve every painful moment from now until eternity." He turned and walked silently to the door.

Tammi watched Grandpa follow him until her father turned around, lifting his hand in a halting motion, before he slipped out. Grandpa's back was to her. His head lowered as his shoulders jolted up and down in quiet sobs.

She lay still as a corpse, uncontrollable tears streaming down her face. She felt as though everything on the inside had been emptied out and only a shell of a broken body remained. She was glad she couldn't speak, because there were no words to say. But oh, how she wished she could sing. Her one refuge was gone.

Tammi was yanked from her state of contemplation when her grandparents placed their hands on her shoulders and began to sing. She felt the vibrato of their voices bounce off the walls inside her hollow, aching chest, filling the emptiness with love and peace. She parted her lips to sing along with them, but not even a grunt came out. She closed her eyes and mouthed the words.

Silas stood unseen at the foot of Tammi's bed. His strong voice mingled with her grandparents' voices, wafting to the heavens as a prayer. Peace like nothing on earth encircled the bed in a protective barrier. Pastor Dave entered the room and quietly slipped down to his knees to pray while the singing continued.

Tammi was still mouthing the words until she realized her grandparents had stopped singing. She opened her eyes to see her grandparents with their heads bowed in prayer. Tammi laid her hand on top of her grandma's.

Her grandma raised her head. "I love you," she whispered.

Tammi nodded and patted her grandma's hand.

"You'll sing again, my sweet," Grandma said. "The Lord didn't give you that beautiful voice to be silent."

Pastor Dave put his arm around Tammi's grandma. "Tammi, there are some friends of yours and Sadie's who want to come and see you soon. Bryce, Krystal, and Mackenzie."

Who was Mackenzie? Another church girl?

Grandma smiled. "Oh, yes. Bryce's family has attended the church for years."

"They wanted me to ask you first. Are you up for that?"

Tammi pointed to a pad of paper on the nightstand. Grandma gave it to her.

Yes, but I want to see Sadie rst

Pastor Dave nodded his head. "I think we can arrange that," he said. "Is that all right with you?" He looked at her grandparents.

"Oh, of course," Grandma said. "I've already spoken with Pam." She turned to Tammi. "Sadie's mother is a wonderful woman."

Pastor Dave smiled. "Okay then. I'll head on over to Sadie's room. That was my next stop." He winked. "I'll be back afterward."

Tammi began writing feverishly, then passed the note to her grandpa.

Did I cause the accident? How bad is Sadie?

Chapter 27

SADIE'S dark lashes fluttered. She squinted from the sunlight that flooded her new room. She breathed in a fresh floral scent. Balloons, cards, and flowers lined the broad windowsill and every available counter space. All the years in foster care of feeling forgotten, and now she was so loved. Yet at the same time, she felt so—*grieved.* How was it possible to feel so conflicted?

She pulled the blanket back and peered at the bandaged stub that used to be her foot. Her thoughts turned to the visit from Lauren and her mother a few days ago.

"Let me pray for you, Sadie," Lauren had said.

Sadie shook her head. "I wish God would've just let me stay in heaven with my real mama," she cried. "Why am I still here?"

Her chest tightened when her mother's eyes glassed over. She really didn't want to hurt her, but the truth was, she was done. Done with this evil world. Done trying to mask her pain. Done putting on a smile.

Done.

Lauren brushed Sadie's long blond hair from her face. "Oh, Sadie," she whispered. "God loves you so much. He let you see your mama is safe with him. But he wants you to *live*. He must have important work for you to do."

Sadie whimpered. "I don't *want* to live anymore. Hasn't there been enough taken away from me? I can't even walk. And I'll never dance again!"

Lauren leaned forward and stared into Sadie's eyes. "You *will* walk and you *will* dance."

Her mother looked at Lauren, then grabbed hold of Sadie's hand. "Yes," she said. "I second that. Sadie, you are the strongest, most courageous person I've ever known." Her mother's lips curled into a quivering smile. "You'll get a prosthetic foot, work hard, and I bet you'll be accepted into Julliard. I'll help you, honey. You can still live your dream."

Lauren and her mom had visited Sadie daily. The two women Sadie most admired in the world had such faith in her—and in God. Did *she* still have faith? She cocked her head to one side, rubbing her hand down her leg. It was so strange. It felt like her foot was still there. But it wasn't. The bandage proved that. No, her foot was gone—forever. What did they do with her foot? Did they just throw it in the trash? She tried to imagine the process. They had to saw it off, right? She cringed and shook her head, willing away the terrible image

Good thoughts. Think good thoughts. The doctor said after some months of healing and therapy, they would fit her for a prosthetic foot. She would have to learn to dance all over again. She imagined herself dancing. Sitting straight up in the bed, she lifted her slim, arms over her head to form a circle. In her mind, she wasn't in a hospital gown. She wasn't in the hospital at all. She was adorned with a white glimmering leotard and feathery wings, just like the angel who took her to heaven. She twirled and leaped through the air.

"Ah-hem."

Sadie's eyes popped open, jolting her from her fantasy.

Pastor Dave stood at her bedside. "Must've been a good dream."

"I was dancing," Sadie said.

Pastor Dave's smile wavered slightly. "That *is* a good one."

"My mom and Lauren think that when I get my prosthetic foot, I'll be able to dance again. Maybe even live my dream of attending Julliard."

Pastor Dave laughed and his eyes crinkled around the edges. "You are a remarkable young woman, Sadie," he said. "I'm going to pray that God helps you achieve that goal."

"Thank you." *I need those prayers because I don't know what I believe anymore.*

"So, I came to find out if you'd be up for a visitor?"

"Who?"

"Tammi wants to see you."

Sadie leaned forward. "Yes! Can you take me to see her? I'd love to get out of this bed."

Pastor Dave pushed Sadie's wheelchair down the hall and around the corner. He stopped and rapped on the door. "Knock, knock. I have a visitor to see you," he said, wheeling her into Tammi's room.

Sadie drew in a sharp breath. There was beautiful Tammi, sitting up in bed, her head wrapped up like a mummy. But Sadie quickly composed herself. *Be positive. Have faith.*

"Tam-m-i-i-i!" she squealed.

Tammi rolled her eyes as usual, a tiny smirk beginning to spread across her bruised face.

I knew it. She does like me!

As Pastor Dave wheeled Sadie closer, she saw Tammi's expression as she zoomed in on Sadie's bandaged leg. Tammi raised her casted wrist to her mouth. She closed her eyes tightly, tears squeezing out the sides. At that moment, Sadie decided that she must have faith for the both of them.

"It's okay, Tammi," Sadie said. She reached out her hand. "Wheel me closer?" she asked Pastor Dave.

Tammi opened her eyes and pointed to the notebook on the nightstand. Sadie craned her neck as she watched Tammi write. "Why can't she speak?"

"She has a traumatic brain injury, which has temporarily affected her speech," said Pastor Dave.

Sadie pulled her hands to her face, making a steeple that covered her mouth. *Oh, God, I need to believe you are here. Please help me to have faith for my friend. She needs you.*

Tammi handed her the note.

I'm sorry about your leg. The doctor says he thinks with time I'll be able to talk again.

Sadie grabbed the pen and began to write when she noticed Tammi shaking her head. Sadie handed her the notebook and pen. Tammi scribbled back.

I can hear you, freak!

Sadie giggled. It felt good. She felt more like herself. "Oh, yeah! Sorry. Well, at least we can tell you're still Tammi in there!"

Pastor Dave laughed too. "I'm going to grab some coffee and let you two visit." Before he reached the door, he turned around glancing at his phone. "I just got a text from Bryce's mom, Shelly. Your friends will be here soon."

"Oh!" Sadie clapped. "I can't wait to see Bry and Krystal!"

Sadie looked at Tammi who was looking down at her lap. "Is it okay with you?"

Tammi shrugged her shoulders then began writing.

I need to know what happened. Is this my fault?

Sadie read the note then looked at Tammi who was staring at Sadie's leg. "Don't blame yourself, Tammi. This is why it's called an accident. I don't know what really happened. The police don't know yet either. All I remember is it was raining cats and dogs. And I remember this enormous angel who took me to heaven."

Tammi's eyes were wide and her mouth hung open. She grabbed the notebook and began scrawling as fast as her hand could go.

I saw a bright light and a huge angel-man by my bed! And he sang to me!!!

Sadie held the notebook in her hand and stared at what Tammi had written, reading it several times. *Oh, thank you, God!* A tear plopped onto the page, smudging the ink. *Maybe I really will dance again.*

She finally looked up, meeting Tammi's scrutinizing glare, then handed her the notepad. Tammi grabbed it and scrawled quickly, revealing one big question mark. Sadie managed a weak smile in response. Tammi raised her pierced brow and pushed the notepad closer.

Sadie chewed her lip, struggling for the right words. "Maybe ..." She looked down at her leg, but quickly looked back at Tammi. She didn't want to lose hope. "Maybe I *will* dance again." Saying it aloud felt good. "And maybe you'll sing again too."

Chapter 28

KRYSTAL jumped when she heard a knock on the bathroom door.

"Krystal, I made a smoothie for you," her mom said loudly. "It's in the frig. I'm going to the gym, okay?" Saturdays were her mom's extended workout days. The other six days she only went for an hour.

"Did you put a little vodka in it?" she mumbled under her breath.

"What?" Her mom asked.

Krystal exaggerated her volume. "Yeah, thanks!" It came out louder and more sarcastic than she intended. *Oh, well. She deserves it.*

Her mom didn't respond. Thank God! Ever since their mother-daughter talk about Krystal's food struggle, her mom had been making her smoothies and asking about her diet. It was extremely annoying. She also scheduled an appointment with one of her psychologist friends.

There was a light wrap on the door. "Krystal, can you come out for a moment?"

Sheesh. What now?

She slapped down her brush on the counter and opened the door. "What?"

"I think we need to have a talk."

"I thought you were going to the gym."

"Well, this is more important," her mom said. "Let's go to my bedroom."

Krystal sluffed behind her mother. She sat down in an overstuffed reading chair and her mother sat on the bed. She watched her mother's face and could tell she was really concentrating on her words. The lines around her eyes and mouth seemed more pronounced lately. She wasn't wearing her usual amount of make-up. Her blond hair was swooshed back tightly in a ponytail.

"Why are you so angry?" Her mother finally asked. Her tone wasn't accusing. She sounded genuine. Still, the question raked on Krystal's nerves.

Krystal snorted. "Are you kidding me?"

"No, I really want to hear from you."

"Uh, let's see. My dad left the house six months ago. Whenever he comes over you find a way to ruin the visit by starting an argument. Why can't you guys work it out?"

Her mom looked glassy-eyed. "It's more complicated than you think."

Krystal interrupted. "Is that why you've been drinking? 'Cause that's another reason I'm angry. And here's one more. You have no right to point the finger at me when you have your own addiction issues." Krystal stood.

"I did not excuse you. Sit down," her mother said.

Krystal ground her teeth and flopped back in the chair.

Her mother cleared her voice. "Krystal, your father is seeing someone else. She's moved in with him."

Krystal stopped breathing. Did someone kick her in the gut? She felt dizzy and sick to her stomach. "How long has he been having an affair?" she managed to whisper.

"Over a year." Her mother looked down, toying with a thread from the quilt. "With *this* one. It's not the first time."

Krystal leaned her head against the back of the chair and let out a long breath. She wanted to scream and call her mom a liar. But the thing was, she *knew*. "I'm so sorry, Mom."

Her mom continued to pick at the quilt. "We tried therapy when it happened the first time." Her voice sounded hollow. "It took a long time for me to trust him again."

"Why haven't you told us? I mean, don't me and the boys deserve to know?"

"I came to that conclusion today," her mom said flatly. "I still need to tell your brothers. But it's—so awful."

Krystal shook her head. "You're setting up an appointment for me to see one of your doctor friends. Maybe you need someone to talk to."

Her mother looked up at Krystal. "I started talking with Pastor Dave. It's been helpful."

Krystal bounced up. "What? You have friends who deal with this kind of crap that are professionals. You're sending me to one, but you don't want to go yourself? What good is a pastor?"

"Pastor Dave has a degree in psychology as well. I trust him *because* he's a pastor. My friends don't look at things from a Biblical perspective which I believe is the source of true wisdom," her mother said. "I didn't make an appointment for you with Dave because I know how you feel about God and church."

"You always told us that religion is for the weak minded. Since when do you believe in this God and church crap?"

Her mother seemed to wince. "Since I realized I've had it all wrong my entire life. Since I realized I'm a messed-up person who needs to be saved."

Krystal frowned. "Saved from what?"

"Saved from my sin and from myself," her mother said. "When your grandma died so suddenly two years ago, I began to question things. Things like, what happens after we die. About six months ago when we were at the Williams' house for dinner, I asked Shelly some tough questions about her church and God. You and Bryce even walked in on that conversation. Do you remember?"

Krystal nodded. "Well, do you really think going to church is going to solve all of this?"

Her mom smiled weakly. "No, but I'm beginning to believe that God can."

"What about the drinking?"

"There's an AA group that meets at church. I started going two weeks ago."

"Wow, it seems the church has everything." Krystal smirked. "If you can go to Pastor Dave, then so should I."

"I'm sure he'd be happy to meet with you," her mom said.

Well, that backfired.

"Whatever," Krystal said. "Are we done now?"

Krystal's mom looked down at her hands that were clasped in her lap. Her expression was strained, like she was holding back tears. "For now, I suppose," she said. "If you want to talk again, please just let me know." She raised her head up. "And I'll set up a time for you to meet with Pastor Dave, okay?"

Krystal shrugged. "Yeah, okay, I guess. He'll probably be better than your stupid doctor friend. Can I go now?"

Her mother nodded, but before Krystal got out the door her

mom called out. "Krystal, I love you."

Krystal stopped, her hand still on the door knob. "Me too," she said without turning around.

KRYSTAL flopped on her bed. It took all of her energy to roll onto her side. She grabbed hold of a stuffed teddy bear from her dad. What she really wanted was to eat—and eat a lot. She could just eat her feelings and puke them out. At least she had control of that. *Right?*

Bulimia hovered just above her with a gruesome sneer, breathing in the scent of her misery and vulnerability. It perched himself on the headboard and began playing on Krystal's cravings. It raised a skeletal arm, making a circular motion that conjured images of mini donuts, cookies, and chips from the box under her bed. Krystal could almost taste them. What would it hurt? Who would know? And what's so terrible about it anyway?

I'm a friggin' healthy athlete! I'll just run it off later!

She climbed off the bed, lay on her stomach and reached for her box of treats but hesitated. She felt her phone vibrating through the pocket of her jeans. She pulled her hand from under the bed and rolled onto her back to check. A text from Bryce. He and his dad had fixed his car and he was on his way over. She jumped up from the floor and ran to the mirror.

She looked awful! Her eyes were bloodshot and her skin looked blotchy. Bulimia moved closer. Digging its claws into her calves, the shriveled little monster gazed up at her, rasping its usual condemnation. "No!" Krystal said aloud. Startled, Bulimia lost its grip and fell backward, landing with a splat on the hardwood floor. It looked up, fear in its bulbous yellow eyes. Directly behind Krystal stood Silas. He had been summoned through the prayers of her mother. His mouth was a straight line across his chiseled face. In his hand was a shimmering sword, raised high and ready to make a blow. Bulimia winced and scrambled under the bed, its skinny arms and legs flailing in every direction, then disappeared in the nick of time.

Chapter 29

MACKENZIE paced back and forth in front of the window. Trey watched from the couch. "Out for coffee with your jock friend again?" he asked.

"I'm going to the hospital to see the girls who were in that accident." She saw a car pull into the driveway. "Gotta go."

Bryce had just stepped out of his custom-built car when Mackenzie walked up. "Hey, there. I was going to come and get you."

Bryce walked around to the passenger side door and opened it. Mackenzie sat down with her hands resting on her bouncing legs. He got in the driver's side and shot her one of his adorable sideways grins. She wondered if he saw her lip quiver when she forced a smile. If he did, he didn't act like it. But then again, he was always the gentleman. A flirty gentleman. *Does he know the effect he has?*

He turned his head over his shoulder as he backed out of the driveway. "Okay, let's go get Krystal."

Mackenzie's legs bounced harder and faster. "Does she know that *I'm* coming?"

Bryce glanced to her then back on the road. "Uh, well. Not exactly," he said. "Hey, I want you to listen to this. It's the youth band from my church." He pushed in a CD and music filled the car.

Mackenzie bit her bottom lip. *Just great.*

"Pretty cool, huh?" He hollered over the music.

Mackenzie had a hard time concentrating on the song. All she could think about was what Krystal would think when she got in the car and saw Bryce and her *together*. She tried to focus on the music. It was pretty good. She looked over at Bryce and nodded her head, trying to force another smile out of her trembling lips.

He nodded back and smiled too, but his was real. "I know, right? Hey, I should play it for Tammi when we see her. I have some songs on my phone." He said excitedly. "What do you think?"

"Uh, sure. But I don't even know her, ya know. I'm just coming along to deliver the cards like you asked."

Bryce smiled, glancing from the road to meet her eyes. "I'm glad you did."

What does he mean?

"Yeah, well, let's hope Krystal is all right with it." She gulped as they pulled into the driveway.

He turned off the engine and unbuckled his seatbelt. "Let me worry about Krystal. She acts like we're married when it comes to me talking to other girls. And she's not even interested in me—at least like *that*. She just likes to toy with me. Like a cat with a bug, ya know?" He smirked, holding his hands upward, shrugging his shoulders. "But that's how we've been for the past few years. I'm used to it." He opened the door, but Mackenzie opened her door at the same time. Bryce's head jerked in her direction.

"I'll go get her," Mackenzie said, hopping out before he could answer.

From the snarl on Krystal's face, Mackenzie could tell this needed explanation—and quickly. "Hey, Bryce invited me to go with you guys."

"I can see that."

"I'm not up to anything," Mackenzie shot back. She heard Krystal's mom holler goodbye from upstairs.

Krystal rolled her eyes. "Whatever. I don't care." She shut the door and leaned her head back against it. "Or maybe I just don't want to deal with this now."

"Stuff's hard with your mom?"

Krystal sighed. "More like my dad *and* mom. I just found out the reason for their separation is because he's having an affair. Oh, and this isn't the first one." She walked past Mackenzie and clomped down the walkway.

Mackenzie hesitated for a moment, shocked that Krystal confided in her. Bryce got out of the car and walked around to the passenger side. Krystal stood in front of the door as if she was used to him opening it for her. Mackenzie climbed into the back seat quietly and looked at the back of Krystal's head as Bryce talked to them both, oblivious of the tension. Or was he? She was getting the idea that Bryce could be using her to make Krystal jealous.

Would Bryce do that? And I don't know what to make of her. Are we friends? I mean why open up about her mom and dad to me? That makes it seem like we're friends, but then she'll go and do something awful. She's got to be the most difficult person on the planet! No wonder Bryce calls her a cat.

"Mackenzie, did you hear me?" Bryce was looking at her through the mirror.

"No, sorry. I guess I spaced."

He laughed. "That's okay. Did you hear the part about Sadie's foot?"

Mackenzie was embarrassed. She really didn't know what he was talking about. Krystal turned around and stared at her. "What are you doing back there? Taking a nap?"

Here she goes again!

Bryce took one hand off the wheel and elbowed Krystal who spun back around. "It's okay, Kenzie," he said. "It's been a hard few weeks for us all."

Krystal mumbled, "Well, that's an understatement." She turned back to Mackenzie again. "Sadie's foot was severed during the accident, I guess. Kind of a big deal."

"Yeah, I just didn't want you to be shocked when you see her. My pastor asked my mom to warn us," Bryce said.

Krystal was still looking at Mackenzie. "I know, it's terrible," she said. "You probably don't know this, but she's a dancer. And the other girl, Tammi, suffered a traumatic brain injury and is unable to speak. And remember, she's a singer." Krystal turned forward now and looked at Bryce.

"What does good 'ole Pastor Dave say about that? I mean what kind of cruel irony is this? Where was God, I ask you?" Krystal's voice got louder. "Oh, and where was this wonderful God when my dad decided to have an affair, and when my mom started drinking?" She turned and looked at Mackenzie. "And when your mom decided to try and end her life. Hmm, where was he then, Bryce?"

Mackenzie's heart was about to jump out of her chest. She saw Bryce's posture stiffen, but he stayed quiet and composed as he pulled the car on the side of the road and parked.

"Your dad had an affair?"

"More than one apparently." Krystal avoided Bryce's stare by looking out the window.

He turned to Mackenzie. "Is what she said about your mom true?"

Mackenzie's chest was tight, like breathing through a straw. Then her mouth began to get watery. Oh, no! She had to get out! "I need out!" Krystal opened the door and leaned forward, so Mackenzie could squeeze out.

The wind washed over her, and she was able to breathe again. She focused on a tree in the yard of the home they'd parked in front of. It was a weeping willow with long branches that swept the ground. It looked sad and hopeless—like she felt. But at least she didn't throw up in Bryce's car.

Krystal got out of the car and stood in front of her, her arms folded across her chest. "I shouldn't have said that. I suck."

Mackenzie shrugged. "You do, but I get it. I wonder the same thing all the time," she said. "About God, I mean."

Bryce approached and stood next to Krystal. "Tammi, Munchkin, and your mom are all alive. What does *that* say about God?" He gazed from Mackenzie to Krystal. "And your mom has been going to church. She *was* an atheist."

Mackenzie looked past them both, staring at the willow tree. She thought about the eerie presence she often felt in her home. *If there was evil, didn't that mean there must be good, too?* "I *do* think there's a God. There's just so much I don't understand," she said.

Krystal raised one brow at Mackenzie, then turned to look at Bryce. "You haven't had to deal with the kind of stuff we have," Krystal said, lifting her chin in Mackenzie's direction. "Your parents are like *Leave It to Beaver* perfect. Your life is perfect and you're perfect."

Mackenzie nodded her head in agreement even though she didn't really know him that well. She trusted what Krystal was saying.

"Look you guys, no one is perfect. We're all messed up. We all have problems and secrets."

"O-o-oh, *secrets*," Krystal said. "What, that your dad caught you watching a porno movie with your meathead jock friends, and you got grounded?"

Mackenzie sucked in her cheeks so she wouldn't smile. Krystal could be so cruel, but that was pretty funny.

The muscles in Bryce's jaw twitched. "You know, Krystal, just because we've been friends all these years doesn't mean you know everything about me."

Friends. Is he in love with her or not? Why doesn't he just get up the nerve and tell her how he really feels. Or maybe he likes their little games.

"Oh, simmer down," Krystal rubbed his bicep. "I know there are some things you've kept hidden. I remember last summer when you came back from that weird church camp thingy all upset. I just never wanted to push you. I'm sorry, Bry. I'm just super confused about God and life and everything. But you *aren't*. It's like there's a storm going on all around you, and you're not even afraid. And I don't get it."

Mackenzie couldn't have said it better. "Yeah, me, too," she shot out, feeling lame when they looked at her.

Bryce pulled his arm free from Krystal's hand, glancing briefly in Mackenzie's direction, then leaned his head back, his Adam's apple protruding. He let out a deep breath to the sky and whispered, "Weird camp thingy." He brought his head back down. "Pastor Dave will be at the hospital. Maybe you two can ask him some questions." Bryce gently pushed away Krystal's hand that rested on his bicep once again. "But right now, we need to stop thinking of ourselves and go see Munchkin and Tammi." He turned around and strolled back to the driver's side of the car.

Mackenzie could see why Krystal called him Mr. Perfect. She rolled her eyes and saw Krystal doing the same thing. "Stop thinking of ourselves," Krystal mimicked in a nasal tone. They both smirked and got in.

Chapter 30

T AMMI looked into Sadie's sparkling eyes. *Where does it come from? How does she have hope even after this?* She thought about Lauren and the same glimmer that always seem to radiate from her. Her grandparents had it too.

"Do you believe me?" Sadie whispered.

Tammi began to write.

Aren't you sad or angry about your foot? You're a dancer!

Sadie glanced at her leg and then back at Tammi. "Yes …"

The door swung opened, and in walked Pastor Dave with Bryce, Krystal, and Mackenzie.

Sadie's head jerked up, catching sight of her friends, she shrieked. "Oh my gosh! It's so good to see you guys!"

Well, that conversation was short-lived.

Bryce got down on his knees near Sadie's wheelchair. His muscular arms encircled her and her chair in a bear hug. Tammi saw Krystal cocking her head to one side to get a glimpse of Sadie's foot. The other girl stood back, closer to Pastor Dave, her eyes wide and glancing around the room. She looked like a scared doe who had just spotted a hunter.

"Krystal!" Sadie squealed.

"Does it hurt?" Krystal asked.

Wow, she doesn't hold back. She's kind of a jerk, but I like it. What does that say about me?

Sadie nodded. "It was really bad the first few days. Now it hurts sometimes at night. And sometimes I still feel my foot. I mean, it feels like I'm moving it and everything. It's really weird."

Sadie looked over at the pale, skinny girl. "Mackenzie, it was really nice of you to come, too."

Tammi rolled her eyes. *How is she always so darn nice?*

She caught Krystal staring at her.

"Hi, Tammi," she said, as if it justified her staring.

Bryce looked at Tammi and smiled. "Man, I'm glad you're okay." He said raking his hands through his dark hair.

Tammi's insides quivered. He was so attractive. But he was a *he*. And he was probably like all other he's. But not the Pastor Dave guy or maybe Lauren's husband, Grant; they seemed special. But this Bryce guy, he was a *he*.

Krystal looked at Tammi's notebook. "How long do the doctors say it will be before you can talk?"

They don't know. They just say they're 'hopeful' I'll speak again

Bryce looked over Krystal's shoulder to read what Tammi had written. Krystal read it aloud for everyone. Hearing Krystal made Tammi angry. She felt powerless and trapped like an animal.

"She's going to sing again and I'm going to dance," Sadie piped in cheerfully.

Tammi clinched her jaw, closing her eyes tightly. She opened them when she heard Krystal speak up.

"How will you dance without your foot?"

Tammi smirked. *She's so harsh! Sadie needs someone like Krystal to bring her back to earth.*

"When I'm healed enough, I can get fitted for a prosthetic foot," Sadie said with smile. "I will have to go to therapy and work really hard. But I lived in more foster homes than I have fingers, so I'm used to hard."

Tammi frowned. *Foster homes. I bet that's where the abuse happened.* Her heart dropped to her stomach thinking of the life Sadie must have had and yet she has faith in God. How?

"How are you so friggin' positive all the time?" Krystal asked. "I'd be so ticked off at God right now!"

Tammi nodded without thinking. Her eyes met with Krystal's momentarily.

Krystal glanced over at Pastor Dave. "Oh, sorry," she said. "But for real."

Sadie shook her head. "I just love you, Krystal. I mean, you just say it like it is. No pretense with you."

"That's for sure," Mackenzie mumbled loud enough to be heard.

Bryce laughed and held up his hand to high five Mackenzie who reluctantly lifted her skinny arm. Krystal slammed her hip into Mackenzie who lost her balance and fell into Bryce. He lost his footing and nearly landed in Sadie's wheelchair.

"Sheesh, don't slam into the girl in the wheelchair!" Krystal said. "You're so mean, Bryce!"

Sadie giggled and snorted, shoving Bryce. "Yeah, you're so mean."

For the first time in days, Tammi felt like laughing. She surprised herself when a garbled grunting noise came out. She covered her mouth with her hand. She'd made small grunts, but this was different.

Bryce looked up at Tammi. "Did you just make a noise? Did you?"

Tammi smiled and nodded her head up and down. Maybe it was good to have them all here.

"See," Sadie said. "She's going to talk again. And she'll sing again too!"

Krystal scowled at Sadie. "Seriously, Sadie, why aren't you ticked?"

The smile left Sadie's face. "I was angry. Really angry. And well, I still get a little mad and feel sorry for myself," she said. "But I cannot stay all sad and angry. I'm still here for a reason. And besides, listen to this you guys. Something amazing happened!" Her face lit up again. "I saw myself above my own body while the doctors were trying to fix my foot. And then I saw this enormous angel that took me to heaven. I heard singing and it was more beautiful than anything I can describe. And then I saw my real mama. She was just as I remember her, except she looked even more lovely and peaceful." Sadie paused to look at her friends.

Tammi glanced at all of their faces. Bryce and Mackenzie were wide-eyed. Krystal had a skeptical frown, but leaned in intently nonetheless. The pastor stood behind them, nodding and smiling.

Sadie continued. "I'm not sure why God didn't let me stay in heaven. But the only thing that makes sense to me is he's got a good reason. I think he wants me to dance again." She rubbed her leg. "I know it must sound crazy. But Tammi saw an angel too, right Tammi?"

Tammi bit her lip. It *was* true. She nodded slowly, expecting the skeptical Krystal to jump all over that—but she didn't. It seemed Krystal had one thing on her mind.

"He wants you to dance again, but you've only got one foot now. How does that make sense? What kind of God does that?" Krystal asked.

"Krystal!" Bryce said.

Pastor Dave looked at Krystal and then at Sadie. "God uses our weakness to display his power and his love. I think you're absolutely right, Sadie."

"Yes!" Sadie said. "I didn't know how to say it, but that's it. I think he wants me to dance again so that I can give him the credit and then other people will find hope!"

"Are you serious right now?" Krystal's voice rose.

Tammi was glad Krystal spoke up because she was more confused than ever. Why would God cause pain in order to bring hope? It seemed downright cruel.

Tammi's doctor stepped in. He spoke with a heavy accent. "I see we have party today." He smiled, his eyes becoming tiny slits. "Good to see you, Pastor, but I must ask you go now. All must go." He motioned his head to the door.

Pastor Dave moved behind Sadie's wheelchair. "I'll take this one back to her room," he said, then looked at Krystal. "You have a lot of valid questions. I'd like to talk with you more. Or any of you." He looked at each face and stopped to look directly at Tammi, causing her insides to twist. "I'll be praying for you. I'll check in with you and Sadie tomorrow after church."

Bryce gave Sadie another hug before Pastor Dave wheeled her out. Krystal, Mackenzie, and Bryce waved goodbye to Tammi. "Maybe we can come back tomorrow too," he said, looking over his shoulder.

Tammi felt the quiet close in on her. She heard their voices grow more distant in the hallway until she couldn't hear them any longer. The doctor had also walked out after checking her charts and machines. It was just her and her thoughts now. She didn't like it. And for good reason.

Incest had been waiting, its scaly body curled under her bed. And it'd brought along some friends, as commanded by Lord Bellian. The shadow of Terror's hulking body blotted out the sunlight that once lit up the room. Anger stood in the opposite corner, puffs of dark smoke pushing out its nostrils. Confusion clung to the ceiling, one of its bulbous eyes looking down at Tammi, the other toward Incest who was sliming its way under Tammi's blanket. The four treacherous beings were licking their lips, ready to inflict all manner of evil, beginning with the obliteration of any shred of faith she may have been entertaining.

Silas and Theo stood just outside of Tammi's room, their faces taut and hands on their swords.

Theo looked to Silas. "There will be a reckoning. The Almighty will prevail."

Silas didn't flinch. "One small prayer. Just one. That's all it will take."

"I'll go see if I can somehow instigate a prayer from Pastor Dave. It may nullify the situation."

"I'd like to nullify them all!" Silas pulled out his sword.

"Stand down, soldier. Those are the orders. I'll return shortly." And with that, Theo vanished, leaving Silas to steam.

Chapter 31

SADIE caught sight of Lauren in the distance down the long hallway. She could hardly contain herself. She wiggled in her chair and waved her arms wildly above her head.

Lauren's distinctive laugh bounced off the walls as she jogged toward Sadie, her sneakers making a splat sound that echoed with every step.

Lauren ran around behind the chair, grabbing hold of the handles while giving Pastor Dave a playful little shove with her hip. "I got it," she said, lifting the front wheels of the chair. "Vroom-vroom."

"She needs to get back to her room soon," Pastor Dave hollered.

"Okay," Lauren said, then whispered into Sadie's ear, "We'll take the long way back."

Sadie squealed. "Hey, I could probably wheel this thing myself, ya know." She turned to look back at Lauren.

Sadie's parents were in the room when Lauren wheeled her in.

"Hi, honey! It's good to see you out and about." Her dad gave her a kiss on the cheek.

Sadie couldn't believe how good she felt after seeing her friends.

"Pastor Dave was telling us about the conversation with your friends in Tammi's room," her mom said.

"I have an idea about that," Sadie looked to Lauren. "Can you come tomorrow and take me back to Tammi's room? I'm going to text Bryce and ask him to bring Krystal and Mackenzie, too."

"Of course," Lauren smiled. "Am I sensing a plan?"

"Yeah, Krystal and Tammi both asked why I'm not angry with God," Sadie said. "I'm not sure about the new girl, Mackenzie, but I know her mom was here in this hospital for several days before being transferred to another clinic."

Lauren nodded, "Yes, we've been praying for her family."

"So, you'll come tomorrow?"

"Sure," Lauren said. "I can talk to Bryce at church tomorrow too."

Sadie's dad helped her back into bed, giving her another kiss. Her mom gently stroked Sadie's face. "We'll go get some dinner and come back for a quick visit before visiting hours are over."

"Maybe bring me back something. I'm tired of this hospital food," Sadie asked.

Her dad gave her a thumbs up. "You got it, kid! How about a hamburger, fries, and chocolate shake?"

Sadie laid her head back on her pillow and closed her eyes. "There is a God!" she teased.

Her dad chuckled and looked to his wife. "I'll take that as a yes."

Everyone said their good-byes just as the doctor and nurse walked in. They told Sadie it was time to change her bandages. She cringed. She'd avoided looking the last time.

The doctor spoke as the nurse began to unwrap. "Sadie, if all looks good with the stump area, a physiotherapist will fit you for a compression garment which will help with the swelling and overall healing. But that won't be until Monday at the earliest."

Stump area. Did he have to say that? Sadie nodded and laid her head back again. She felt a wave of nausea come over her. She wanted to look when the nurse had all the bandages off, but her stomach wouldn't allow it. Her mouth was filling with saliva.

"I feel sick." Sadie said.

The nurse grabbed a basin.

Once the dressing had been changed and she was finished being a human pin-cushion, the doctor and nurse left her to rest. But rest wasn't coming. She was restless and in pain, but worse was the heavy feeling that was nearly suffocating her. A familiar presence Sadie could sense.

Fear, her unwanted companion, had been waiting for a moment of vulnerability and now joined her in the bed, winding its snake-like tail around her head like a scaly turban. He brought a partner, Anxiety, who wrapped itself around Sadie's leg near the bandages, squeezed tightly.

Sadie's heart was pounding, and she began to hyperventilate, tears streaming down her cheeks. She squeezed her eyes shut. *Think good thoughts. Think good thoughts.* In her mind, Sadie was with her mama in heaven. Fear squeezed her head tighter and tighter and Sadie fought to focus.

She remembered a Bible verse her mother told her after a nightmare. *Perfect love casts out all fear.* Drawing in a deep breath, she opened her eyes.

"You're with me, God," she whispered. Fear and Anxiety lost their grip and fell to the floor, writhing in pain.

Sadie whispered another Bible verse. "I will never leave you nor forsake you." Then another; this time louder. "I will fear no evil, for you are with me." She regained her strength and propped herself up on her elbows. "Evil, that's what this is." She felt the conflict between fear and peace. Her arms began to shake and grow weaker.

A much larger demon, Terror, entered the room and hovered over the bed. It flapped its membranous wings and a burst of acrid air forced Sadie's hair back.

Silas appeared, lifting his sword and slashing through the demon. Terror yelped, a piece of its wing dripping with blood. Silas wielded his sword once again, but Terror had evaporated into a cloud of ashy smoke. The other two demons had vanished the moment Silas entered.

Sadie felt peace wash over her, warmth filling the room. The evil was gone! She sat up and exclaimed, "For every child of God defeats this evil world, and we achieve this victory through our faith."

How did I remember those Scriptures? Oh, God, you really are with me!

Silas sheathed his sword, then knelt in a prayer of thanksgiving. At least he was empowered to help *this* one. But the attack proved the demons were increasing in number and in strength every day.

Chapter 32

KRYSTAL rubbed the sleep from her eyes. She breathed in the tantalizing aroma of coffee and, could it possibly be ... *bacon?* Most likely it was turkey bacon at her house, but oh, well. She threw the comforter from her legs and scuffed into the kitchen.

Kory and Kamron were at the table discussing plays for JV football as usual. They were all dressed and looking much too awake. Krystal shook her head in disgust and moved deliriously closer to the coffee pot. The yellow curtains were pulled back, allowing sunlight to stream into the room. She squinted, feeling like Dracula at sunup. *Stupid sun.*

Her brothers chuckled behind her. "Why are you up so early on a Sunday, K?" Kamron asked.

"Coffee and bacon, duh."

Her mom was at the stove making scrambled eggs. "I'm glad you're up. This is almost finished." She sounded irksomely cheery. *They all did.*

Krystal held her coffee in one hand and snagged a slice of turkey bacon with the other. She sat down on the edge of the chair, nearly falling off. Her coffee sloshed out the side of the cup, hitting her wrist. Krystal let out a curse word. Her brothers erupted in laughter. Her mother spun around.

"I'm fine," Krystal said, grabbing a napkin. "Why are you all so cheery? It's zero-dark-thirty on a friggin' Sunday morning, for Christ's sake!"

Her brothers were snorting and falling all over themselves. "It's nine o'clock, Krystal," Kory managed to say between wheezes and snorts.

Her mother sat down next to her, taking hold of her wrist to make sure she was all right. "That's exactly the reason, Krystal. For Christ's sake."

She snatched her wrist from her mother's grip and stood up. "Are you kidding me?" she said, then mimicked. "For Christ's sake."

Her brothers weren't laughing anymore. Krystal grabbed her coffee, and slice of bacon and left. As she headed back up to her room she heard the hushed voices of her mother and brothers. She put her foot on the first step and paused to see if she could hear what they were saying, but couldn't. They were whispering. *Ugh!*

She set her coffee on the step, stuffed the bacon in her mouth and edged closer to the kitchen. She heard Kamron's baritone voice. "Please God," he said. "Help our sister see that you are real and that you care about her so much."

They're praying for me!

She frowned, drawing in her bottom lip. She wanted to be angry, but she just couldn't. She pushed her hair behind her ear as if that would help her hear better, tilting her head toward the kitchen.

"God, I pray for Dad. He needs you." Kasey now. "And I pray that you help Mom stay strong and sober."

They know about the drinking and about Dad. And they're like totally supporting Mom.

Next, she heard her mother's voice. She couldn't understand everything. She could tell by the sniffing that her mother was crying. All she could make out was, "Thank you that you have forgiven me and given me a chance to make things right."

Krystal moved closer, her back against the wall. The prayers of her family continued. Her legs began to shake as she slowly slid down the wall. She grasped her knees to her chest, lay her head on them and wept.

She quickly shot up when she heard a chair slide across the kitchen floor.

Her mom came out of the kitchen and jumped back when she caught a glimpse of Krystal from the corner of her eye. "Oh! You scared me."

She looked at her mother's worn face and couldn't hold it together. She moved closer and fell into her mother's open arms. "I'm so sorry. I'm so, so sorry," she sobbed.

"Oh, honey," her mom whispered. Krystal breathed in her mother's vanilla scent. She didn't realize how much she missed being held.

Krystal pulled back a bit, still holding her mom. "All I've been doing is thinking of myself and how hard this has been for me. And you—this has been so bad for you."

Kamron and Kasey came around the corner, drawing in close. Kamron put his arm around his sister's shoulder, and Kasey put his around their mom's. Silas towered over them, his hefty arms raised high, summoning Theo and a few other angels to join him in ousting the wicked creatures who were closing in, scheming to break up the family prayer.

Anger pushed past Bulimia and Alcoholism but stopped short at the presence of the mighty angels. It snorted, both heads puffing dark smoke that encircled the family. Confusion moved in and began fanning the smoke. Anger glared at Silas and took a step closer. Bulimia snickered and inched its way up just behind Anger. Silas and Theo unsheathed their swords, the whistling sound halting Anger's move to attack. It shrank back, the dark slits in its yellow eyes growing wide. The massive angels empowered with the prayers and love of the family sent each hidden slimy, scaly, and contorted creature screeching and melting into a thick tar-like ooze from every nook and cranny of the house. Their cries resounded in the heavenlies but were drowned out by the cheers of Silas, Theo, and several other angelic beings.

Krystal shuddered, unaware of the battle that had taken place and yet sensing it at the same time. "Something's different," Krystal said. "It's so weird. I feel *lighter* somehow. Does that sound stupid?"

Even her mom's face looked better. Her eyes were bright, and the dark circles seemed to have disappeared.

"It doesn't sound weird, honey," her mom smiled. "It sounds like God."

Krystal tilted her head to the side and looked into her mother's face. Mom really meant what she was saying. She looked to Kamron and Kasey now. They believed it too.

"You guys really think that God cares about all of our crap?" Krystal asked, scanning each of their faces. "Kamron? Kasey?"

They both nodded, but Kamron spoke up. "I know you may not want to hear this, Krystal, but why don't you come to church and see?"

"So the way God cares about you is if you go to church?" she said with an edge to her voice.

"No, he cares about everyone. But the best way to learn about him is in church and the Bible," Kasey chimed in. Her mother and Kamron nodded in agreement.

Krystal bit her lip and sighed. "But there's so much that doesn't make sense. Does he care about Sadie and that she lost her foot in an accident and can't dance now? I mean, hasn't her life been hard enough with being in foster care?"

Her mom spoke. "Krystal, there are lots of things in this life that don't make sense. Believe me, I've been searching for answers. I just know that for the first time I have real peace despite my circumstances."

Krystal looked at her. "I believe you, Mom," she said. "I just don't know if I trust a God who lets all this bad stuff happen."

"I think you should talk to Lauren at church. Or Pastor Dave," Kamron said.

Kasey folded his arms across his chest, his biceps looking more pronounced, reminding Krystal how mature her brothers had become. "Yeah, Grant and Lauren are the youth leaders. Pastor Dave is cool, but I think you'd like Lauren."

Kamron nodded in agreement.

"Have you two talked with them?" Krystal asked.

"Yeah," they said in unison.

Krystal shrugged and looked down at her raggedy slippers. Could it be that easy? Then she thought of Bryce and how he'd changed over the past year. And Sadie who'd been given the poopy end of the stick in life and still seemed to have so much *hope*.

Krystal's pajama pocket started to vibrate. She glanced at her phone. Bryce.

I know you're probably still asleep now, but Sadie asked if we could come back today. I'll be over after church to pick you up.

205

Just then Krystal began to formulate a plan. She stuffed the phone back in her pocket. She gave her mom another hug. "I love you," she said then looked at her brothers. "Thanks for talking with me. I'm going to go back to bed for a while."

She laid down on her bed, pulled the comforter over her head and soaked in the warmth and coziness—temporarily. She relished the last few minutes of sweet slumber until she heard her mom and brothers pull out of the driveway. Then she hopped out of the bed and stood gazing in her closet.

What's appropriate church attire, I wonder?

She felt giddy just thinking of the looks on her family's—and Bryce's faces. She kind of felt like Ebenezer Scrooge on Christmas morning.

Chapter 33

MACKENZIE put the last barrel curl in her hair and stood back. Pleased, she tidied up the bathroom and walked by Harper's room. The door was open, so she went in.

Harper was standing in front of her closet. "I don't know what to wear," she said looking over her shoulder. "Is it okay to wear jeans? You're wearing them."

"Bryce told me that everyone is really casual except for some of the old folks," Mackenzie said. "I'm still surprised Dad agreed to go to church."

"Yeah, I know. It's a good sign." Harper held up her jeans. "But these are okay?"

"Just wear what's comfortable," Mackenzie shrugged. "Besides, you always look good." She moved closer to her sister, grabbing a strand of her hair and twirling it between her fingers.

Harper smirked. "Hmmm, you're lookin' pretty good yourself. Is that for Bryce?"

Mackenzie felt the usual red blotches starting on her chest and moving up her neck. She rolled her eyes, trying to appear unfazed. "No." Mackenzie turned around. "I'm going to check on Del and get some breakfast."

"Uh-huh, r-i-i-ight."

Mackenzie turned back to face Harper. "Bryce and Krystal are both my friends. I can tell that they have a thing for each other and I'd never come between that." *At least I think they're my friends.*

Harper stepped back. "Sorry. I just thought. Well, he *is* picking you up, right?"

Mackenzie took her hands from her hips, and rested them at her sides, releasing a sigh. "It's all right, Harper. Yeah, Bryce did offer to pick me up. That's just how he is. He's always a gentleman." She brought her hand up to her mouth, nibbling at her nail. "I do think he's cute. And funny. And nice. But, he's taken."

Harper smiled and shrugged.

Mackenzie turned to walk out, speaking over her shoulder, "Hey, maybe he can introduce me to one of his church friends because there are *no* good guys at school, that's for sure."

She looked at the clock on the microwave just as the doorbell rang and hollered to her family. "It's getting late. You guys better get a move on! Bryce is here. I'll see you guys there." She turned around and smacked right into Trey.

"Sheesh! I can hear you," Trey said. "Better get the door for Loverboy."

Mackenzie shoved past him and opened the door.

Bryce smiled. "We're still early. Wanna stop at the coffee shop?"

"I can always go for coffee," Mackenzie said as she shut the door.

When they parked at the coffee shop, Mackenzie unbuckled the seatbelt, ready to get out.

"Hold up a minute. I wanna ask you something, Kenzie." Bryce's voice was a little shaky. "Uh, how's your mom?"

Mackenzie took her hand off the door handle and stared at her lap. "She—" her voice cracked. "She's at a different hospital now."

Bryce was staring at her. "That's probably a good thing, right?"

She nodded, still looking at her hands in her lap. For some stupid reason, she could feel tears threatening to spill down her cheeks. She looked out the window then turned when he put his hand on her shoulder and found herself staring straight into those caring eyes.

"Oh man, I didn't mean to make you sad. I'm sorry. Come here." He pulled her into his arms.

Mackenzie melted. She could feel his warm breath on her ear. Her skin got all goosepimply. She breathed in staggered breaths, trying not to cry anymore, but it was no use. The floodgate had opened. Bryce just held her, rubbing her back and whispering, "It'll be okay."

Oh, what is happening? I should pull away, but I don't want to.

When she finally gathered the strength to pull away, Bryce didn't. He kept his arms around her, staring into her eyes, drawing closer until his lips brushed hers ever so softly. Mackenzie closed her eyes then quickly opened them. Bryce smiled and wiped a tear from her face with his thumb, then kissed her cheek.

"Bryce, we can't do this," she said, leaning backward and out of his embrace.

He didn't wait for an answer. "It's because of Krystal, right?"

She nodded. "I can tell you two have a thing. I'm not getting in the way of that."

Bryce shook his head. "It's like I told you. She plays games with me. She's got to know what's she's doing. It's like she's a frozen fire. She's driving me crazy!"

Mackenzie cut him off. "So, is that what this is? A new game?"

Bryce's eyes quickly darted away. "I'm sorry," he said looking out the window. "This was a jerk thing to do. I mean, I like you, Mackenzie." He was looking at her now. "But, but ..."

"But you love Krystal?"

"What does it matter? She doesn't want me like that."

Mackenzie's stomach churned. She could feel acid making its way up her throat. "Let's skip the coffee and get to church, okay?"

Bryce nodded and started the engine. They rode in silence until they arrived in the parking lot. Then Bryce finally looked at her.

"I *do* like you, Mackenzie," he said before opening his door.

Mackenzie didn't respond. She hurried to get out before Bryce came around to her side to be his typical gentleman-self and open the door for her. She bolted like a wild mustang, never turning back. And he didn't come after her.

Thanks, a lot, Bryce Williams! Now I don't know what I feel.

Mackenzie caught sight of her family and ran to catch up with them. They walked in and were greeted by Bryce's mom, who guided them to seats behind hers. When Bryce trailed in, he sat next to his mom just in front of Mackenzie. He turned around and gave her a weak smile. She looked away. Bryce got up and sat in the empty seat next to her. He gave a nod to Trey, who sat on the other side of Mackenzie.

"So, I'm going to pick up Krystal after church for lunch then go over to the hospital again," Bryce said. "Do you want to go?"

So, I'm supposed to go on like normal?

A muscle in Bryce's jaw twitched and his eyes pleaded with her.

"So, you've already asked Krystal?" she finally said.

A voice came from behind her. "Asked Krystal what?"

Mackenzie spun around. *Krystal!*

Before Mackenzie could respond, Bryce had Krystal wrapped in one of his bear hugs. She heard him speak softly. "I'm so happy you're here. I've been praying for this."

The two stood interlocked for what Mackenzie thought was an embarrassingly long time. And she was more confused now than ever.

"I need to find my family." Krystal dropped her arms, but Bryce kept his around Krystal's waist. "They don't know I'm here."

Bryce's eyes grew wide. "Oh, wow! Your mom's gonna flip," he said. "I'll help you find her." He took a few steps, then turned back to Mackenzie. "Oh sorry, Kenzie. We'll be back soon."

Mackenzie hoped her smile looked more genuine than it felt. "You know where I'll be."

I guess it was a game.

The next thing she knew, a band started to play and the awkward introductions ceased as everyone took their seats. Krystal sat next to Bryce, directly in front of Mackenzie. She wasn't sure, but it seemed like they were holding hands. She tilted her head and leaned into Trey. Yep, they were definitely holding hands! Krystal may act like a cat, but *he's* a dog!

When the service ended, people scurried about, some standing around in little clusters to visit. It reminded Mackenzie of what the kids at school did. Her dad was talking with Bryce's parents. Harper, Trey, and Del were talking with Krystal's brothers. And there she stood pretending not to be bothered by Krystal and Bryce who were engrossed in each other, when Bryce must have felt her gaze and turned in her direction.

Mackenzie's eyes darted down at her phone when she heard him say, "So, can I interest you two lovely ladies in lunch?"

So, should I tell Krystal that you kissed me?

Mackenzie kept looking at her phone. "Uh, maybe." She needed a diversion and fast. "Where's the restroom?" she asked, still toying with her phone.

"I need to go too. You go mingle with all your churchy peeps." Krystal waved her hand, shooing Bryce, then did a head wave for Mackenzie to follow.

Mackenzie's didn't move right away. She followed Krystal's back, weaving through the crowds. Then she turned to give Bryce the most serious glare she could muster. He shrugged, his lips mouthing, *I'm sorry,* before walking away, tail between his legs! *Yeah, a sorry, pathetic, flirty dog!*

Mackenzie followed Krystal through the maze of people until she noticed a sign for the restroom. Krystal turned. "I'm surprised to see you here."

"Yeah, I could say the same thing. It's weird you'd show up on my first day here."

Krystal motioned to an adjacent door marked *Powder Room* and held the door open for Mackenzie. She glanced around the quaint room with pink flowered wall paper. There was a small couch, two fancy wing-backed chairs and coffee table with flowers that matched the walls. With no one else in the room, Mackenzie chose to sit in one of the fancy chairs.

Krystal sat in the other and leaned forward, her hands on her lap. "What do you think of all this church stuff?"

Mackenzie frowned. "Wait. Are we like friends now? Because I can't figure you out."

Krystal looked away, then back. "Well, I thought so. I *hope so*, I mean."

Mackenzie pushed away what had happened between her and Bryce. Best not to say anything. She knew for sure that he wouldn't. "I want to believe that we're done with all the competition stuff and that you really want to be friends."

"Look, I'm not close to anyone but Bryce and his family."

"Oh come on," Mackenzie shot back. "You're super popular. You know everyone at the entire school."

"I'm sure you've figured out that I'm not really a 'people' person. So, I can't fathom why they even like me. I'm sarcastic and mean, but they still come around."

Mackenzie agreed. "That's true."

Krystal shook her head, a smirk spreading across her lips. "See what I mean, you *get* me. And besides that, you know more about me than any of those people at school. I can't be real with them. They're so immature and stupid." She sighed. "I mean come on, we both know each other's secrets. We've kind of been through a lot."

Mackenzie nodded. "Okay, if we're friends, then let's talk about this church stuff. What did you think of Pastor Dave's sermon-talk thingy?"

"Okay, that's what I wanted to talk about," Krystal leaned forward, tucking her long hair behind her ears. "Honestly, it scared me."

"Me too." Makenzie's eyes widened. "He said that our battle is not against flesh and blood, but with evil powers. And you know what? I *believe* him."

"Me too." Krystal's pupils grew large.

Mackenzie leaned in closer, almost whispering. "I think there are some kind of dark forces that try to scare us and play on all our fears." She swallowed. "I've *felt* it before."

Krystal's head bobbed up and down. "I know what you mean. But why does God—if he exists—let that happen?"

"Oh, God exists." Of that, Mackenzie was certain. "How else can there be evil things if there aren't good things too? And I felt the good in this place today. Didn't you?"

Krystal toyed with her necklace, looking down at the pink carpet. "I came today because I heard my mom and brothers praying for me this morning. At first, they didn't know I was listening. I can't explain it, but something happened." She glanced up. "I just decided it was time to see what this is all about, I guess." She pulled her phone from her pocket. "Bryce is asking if we fell in. We better go."

"Wait," Mackenzie said. "One more thing. The priest—I mean pastor—asked if we know where we'd go if we died today. Like heaven or hell, I guess. What do you think?"

Krystal stood up, shaking her head. "I don't know. What do you think?"

Mackenzie stood, her thin arms folded tightly across her chest, shrugged and headed toward the door.

Krystal called out to her. "Oh, you're going with us to the hospital after lunch, right?"

Mackenzie stopped walking and turned to face Krystal. "Yeah, I guess I'll go. Oh, by the way, my mom's not there anymore. She's finally where she needs to be. It's a special hospital for the mentally ill."

Krystal bit her lower lip and frowned. "I'm sorry." She actually seemed to mean it.

"It's probably for the best. Maybe she'll finally get the help she needs."

"I hope so," Krystal said with more sincerity than Mackenzie thought she could handle without tears.

"Thanks," she whispered. "Hey, wait. Was Bryce holding your hand?"

Krystal's eyes sparkled. "Yes!" She nearly squealed like Sadie.

Mackenzie gulped. Bryce had only kissed her to make Krystal jealous, *right?*

Chapter 34

TAMMI quickly tried to smooth down the tendrils of loose hair from the bandage around her forehead, while leaning forward to see who was entering her room.

Sadie's cheery voice proceeded her. "We-e-e-e're he-e-e-e-ere!"

Lauren wheeled Sadie up close to the bed. Tammi surprised even herself, realizing the excitement that bubbled inside when she saw the guitar strap on Lauren's shoulder. Tammi had admired the guitar when she first met Lauren. It was a beautiful Martin with rosewood on the sides and back. It had a unique warm tone that complimented Lauren's alto voice. Tammi had been saving for over a year to buy a new guitar. Would she even need it now?

"I brought the music. We can get the party started." Lauren gave an exaggerated wink in Tammi's direction.

Tammi reached for her notebook. The hospital gown slipped to the side of her bony shoulder, showing her tattoo. She tugged at the gown as quickly as possible to cover herself and began writing.

Thanks for coming. I can't wait to hear you play. I'm desperate for music!!!

Sadie read the note. "Hey, what am I, chopped liver?" With a limp arm, she handed it to Lauren.

Tammi felt a laugh trying to make its way out of her mouth. Instead, all that came was a few staggered caveman grunts. But it was the most she'd been able to manage since the accident.

Sadie squinted her eyes and pointed at Tammi as if she was a child caught with their hand in the cookie jar. "I heard that! See, you'll be talking in no time!"

Tammi sighed at the minuscule step of progress. If she couldn't even laugh, how would she ever sing again?

"Oh, and the others are on their way. Bryce just texted me like ten minutes ago," Sadie said.

Just then the door opened. "Well, speak of the devil," Sadie giggled. "Oops!" She noticed it was Pastor Dave. "Sorry. I thought you were ..."

Bryce popped his head around Pastor Dave. "Me!" He hollered, skidding across the slick floor on his heels.

Talk about making a grand entrance. Man, this guy loves attention!

"Did she say devil? That's most likely *me*," Krystal said.

Mackenzie followed behind Krystal making devil horns with her fingers over the top of Krystal's head. When she turned around sharply, Mackenzie just shrugged, her eyes darting from side to side innocently. Tammi smirked, and this time a bark like a seal came out. She covered her mouth with her hands. The once stale and quiet room now was full of life and laughter.

Tammi gazed at each face, feeling strangely connected. These people actually cared enough to take time out to see her. She felt a lump form in her throat. She gulped, willing herself not to get emotional. Luckily, Lauren began to play her guitar, which helped her to relax. Soon Sadie, the pastor, and Bryce were singing along. Even though Tammi only recognized a few of the songs—because they were church ones—she could still imagine singing harmony. She listened, longing to be a part of it.

God, if you're really there, please give me my voice back. I don't just want to sing. I want to sing like Lauren does. And my grandpa does. I want whatever it is they have.

During the next song, Tammi noticed Bryce and Krystal slip out the door, while everyone else continued to sing. When the song was almost over, Krystal came back in without Bryce. Her eyes were focused on Mackenzie whose color had completely left her face.

Lauren strummed her final note and Sadie spoke up. "Where's Bry?" She asked, looking at Krystal.

Krystal kept staring at Mackenzie while she answered Sadie. "I don't know," she said flatly.

Tammi sensed a chill between the two girls. Pastor Dave seemed to notice it too. He stood announcing he'd go look for Bryce.

Uh-oh. This seems serious.

BRYCE joined his parents, Tammi's grandparents, and Grant in the hospital chapel. Everyone waited for Pastor Dave, who had suggested this meeting after the morning service. After a quick greeting and a nod in Bryce's direction, the pastor suggested everyone pull their chairs into a circle.

Little lines and creases showed at the sides of his eyes as Pastor Dave looked at his friends and prayer partners. "I believe God is using all four of these girls' tragic pasts and current situations— including the accident—to draw each of them to his love. I also know the devil wants to keep them confused, hurting, and in the dark. But God knows just what will draw them to his light. God, and only God, can use what the enemy means for evil and turn it into good. And we have the privilege to be God's instruments by loving them and praying for them."

"I couldn't have said it better, Pastor." Tammi's grandpa said, and put his arm around his wife's small frame.

Pastor Dave nodded, bowed his head, and began to pray. "Father God, we know you are in control of all things. You have brought these four girls together for a divine purpose. We pray that you hold back the devil and his demons. Use Lauren to bring your message of hope to Tammi, Sadie, Krystal, and Mackenzie. In the powerful name of Jesus!"

As the group huddled together, the prayers continued. Each prayer rose like glimmering specks of stardust that floated upward through the ceiling, resonating throughout the heavenly realm. A multitude of angels watched with joy as the prayers landed in a golden bowl that sat in front of a golden altar before the throne of God Almighty.

As the prayers entered the bowl, smoke was released. An enormous angel, larger than Philo, with wings that were covered with hundreds of human-like eyes, towered near the sacred golden bowl of prayers. He held a censer, into which he scooped flaming coals from the altar. He hurled the contents from the censer to the earth causing peals of thunder, rumblings, flashes of lightning, and an earthquake.

Silas, Philo, Theo, and twenty other angels flew like comets, intersecting with the fiery coals hitting the earth's atmosphere faster than the speed of sound. They were empowered and ready for the battle ahead.

TAMMI gnawed on her lip. Krystal, looking like she was about to erupt, stepped close to Mackenzie who in turn, took a step back. By the look on Sadie and Lauren's faces, they'd also figured out the hot lava of Krystal's wrath was about to invade the room.

"I thought we were friends." Krystal inched even closer to Mackenzie who had gone back as far as she could go—right into the side of Tammi's bed.

Tammi toyed nervously with her eyebrow piercing. *Great, a ringside seat. Where's the popcorn?*

Krystal's face contorted. "Why didn't you tell me what he did? You *had* the opportunity."

Mackenzie looked down at her feet. "I can't believe he actually told you."

"*You* should have told me!"

Mackenzie's head shot up. "I'm not to blame here. I told him to stop."

Lauren stepped in beside Krystal. "Okay, girls. Let's sit down and talk about this calmly."

Krystal's head spun in Lauren's direction. "*Let's?* You aren't involved here. So back off lady."

Lauren stood up straight as an arrow, hands on her hips. "*You* involved us when you brought this into the room. Now sit." Her voice was calm, but authoritative.

Krystal sat down. Lauren sat next to her, and Mackenzie sat next to Lauren.

Tammi scrawled quickly in her notebook, then handed it to Sadie who read it aloud.

Look, I barely know Bryce, and I can see he's a big flirt. You guys don't need him.

Mackenzie frowned at Tammi, then looked away. "Krystal, Bryce was playing a game to make you jealous. He *does* really love you," she said, looking at Krystal and then the others and back at Krystal again. "I should have told you, but I didn't want to hurt you. It seemed you two had finally admitted your feelings for each other. And he told me he was sorry." Mackenzie picked at the skin on the sides of her nails. "Besides, it was embarrassing to be used like that. Can we just move on?"

"I don't know how to feel right now," Krystal said. "I've wanted him to love me for so long. But I've also wanted a real friend. One I could trust. I *thought* I found one."

"You did," Mackenzie whispered, her eyes filling with tears.

Tammi reached for her notebook again. *I knew that Bryce was trouble! I should tell them how flirty he was with me. On second thought—nope.* She put the pen down without writing a word.

Krystal turned her head away, wiping a tear from her eye. Everyone sat speechless. Sadie fiddled with her blanket, Mackenzie starred at the floor, and Lauren sat stiffly with her hands folded together in her lap.

Tammi took in a deep breath. *This is why I'm not close to people. They are just way too complicated. How did I get into this?*

The awkward silence was interrupted when Krystal turned to Lauren. "Why is life so hard? I just don't get why God—if there is a God—allows so much pain."

A knot formed in Tammi's throat. She knew exactly what Krystal was saying. And for some reason, she felt extremely anxious and hot. She lifted her hand to her face to smooth away the tiny beads of sweat from her forehead.

Sadie noticed something was wrong. "Are you okay, Tammi? Do you want some water?"

Tammi took a strenuous gulp, nodding her head. Krystal rolled her eyes at Sadie struggling to reach the water pitcher on the nightstand. She stood, poured the ice water into a Styrofoam cup, and handed it to Tammi.

Dang it! Tammi's hand shook as she reached for the cup. By Krystal's raised eyebrow, Tammi knew she noticed but rather than say anything, she looked at Lauren again. *Whew!*

"Uh, so why is God such a jerk?" Krystal continued.

Lauren set her guitar up against the wall and dragged her chair closer to the bed. She looked at Krystal first, then everyone else. "I'll get right to the point." She cleared her throat. "All right, so I know that there's been some difficult questions about God coming from each of you, right?"

There was a rap on the door. Bryce poked his head in. Lauren stood up and walked toward him. "Bry, we'll text you when it's safe to come in, okay?" She went back to her seat.

Bryce looked at Krystal. "I'll text you later," she said.

He sucked in his lower lip, emphasizing his dimples, nodded and closed the door.

Tammi wished she could get a good look at Krystal's expression, but she didn't want to lean forward and stare like Sadie was doing. Her question was answered when Krystal's head swiveled in Sadie's direction revealing a stone-cold stare.

Krystal shot up like a bottle rocket, her chair wobbling from side to side. "If this is some kind of religious intervention crap, I'm leaving."

Mackenzie got out of her chair and faced Krystal with her arms folded across her chest. "Who said anything about intervention or religion? You *do* have questions, right?" She didn't wait for a shocked Krystal to answer. "I mean we both do. Look, Krystal, you said yourself that we know each other's secrets. Things that no one else knows. I'm sorry about Bryce. It's obvious he cares or he wouldn't dare come back in here. But are we friends or not?"

Krystal starred at the floor, sucking in her quivering bottom lip. She nodded without looking at Mackenzie.

"Okay then," Mackenzie said calmly. "Let's put aside the stuff with Bryce. We can see that this God stuff has helped Sadie and even Bryce."

Sadie looked like a bobble head doll. "Uh-huh, it's true."

Mackenzie continued. "Let's listen to her, okay?"

The room had that quiet-before-the-storm feel. Krystal and Mackenzie stood, still facing each other without saying a thing. Tammi noticed that Lauren's lips were moving slightly. *Praying. Just like my grandparents.*

Krystal swiveled toward Lauren. "Yeah, I *do* have questions." She placed her hands on her hips, scowling down at her. "I suppose my mom talked with you. She's the new convert." Krystal's voice was mocking. "Let me guess, you were bulimic when you were a teen, too. Oh, and you probably came from a divorced family of alcoholics."

Uh-oh. More secrets. We are a screwed-up bunch!

Lauren looked up at Krystal squarely. "No. Your mom didn't talk to me. But she gave Pastor Dave permission to. And no, I don't have a history of bulimia, alcoholism, or divorce," she said calmly. "But I *do* know sexual abuse, low self-esteem, battling negative thoughts, anger to the point of hate, dealing with evil forces, and blaming God. *And* I think I can help each of you with your questions."

Krystal took one wobbly step backward, flipped her longs bangs back, and then sat back down. "Okay," she said. "You've got my attention."

Tammi swallowed hard. *And mine too.*

Chapter 35

The Spirit of the Sovereign LORD is upon me,
for the LORD has anointed me
to bring good news to the poor.
He has sent me to comfort the brokenhearted
and to proclaim that captives will be released
and prisoners will be freed.
He has sent me to tell those who mourn
that the time of the LORD's favor has come,
and with it, the day of God's anger against their enemies.
To all who mourn in Israel,
he will give a crown of beauty for ashes,
a joyous blessing instead of mourning,
festive praise instead of despair.
In their righteousness, they will be like great oaks
that the LORD has planted for his own glory.
Isaiah 61:1-3 NLT

Silas, Philo, and Theo stood on either side of Lauren. Their massive shimmering shields were raised as a covering over her and the four girls. An additional twenty of God's angels stood stalwartly around and outside the room, swords unsheathed, sandaled feet planted firmly and ready. Demons swooped overhead, screaming blasphemies and threats.

"You'll never be free! You're worthless! Ugly! Disgusting tramp!" They hissed, wings nearly swiping the girls' faces.

God's angels moved with speed and accuracy. The deafening screeches were met with a collision of swords, claws, and shields obliterating the smaller and less powerful demons right away. Flaming arrows whizzed through the air, but nothing could penetrate the iron ceiling of protection provided by the angels' shields over the girls.

A loud trumpet blast pierced through the chaotic chants and screams. Anger, Lust, Bulimia, Shame, Incest, Oppression, Depression, and Anxiety halted in mid-air. Something was *different*. Their usual tactics were ineffective. They knew there was real cause for worry when Lord Bellian descended with a thunderous crash and landed in a heap on the floor. Theo pushed a strand of dark hair from his face, his fiery eyes glaring down at Bellian, sword raised, ready to strike again.

Bursts of light sparked like fireworks and rained down shimmering droplets upon the evil horde sending them swirling straight through the ceiling. Their shrieks, moans, and cries rumbled throughout the heavenlies. Defeat was imminent.

The time for freedom had finally come.

All four girls stared at Lauren. She situated herself in the chair, with no idea of the magnitude of the battle that had taken place in this very moment.

"For years I kept it a secret. For years, I listened to the voices in my head telling me I was dirty, ugly, unwanted, unlovable, and alone. Voices that said that no one would understand or could help me." Lauren paused, looking intently at each set of frightened eyes staring into hers.

"I know what it feels like to be a prisoner in your own mind. I know what it's like to live in fear, shame, and guilt. And I also know about anger. Anger at myself and God for letting it happen. Anger at my parents for not protecting me." Lauren's trembling voice trailed off.

"I'm so ticked!" Krystal hollered. She clenched her fists and cursed God.

Lauren nodded. "I see it in each of you. You're all hurt, angry, and afraid. But I'm here to help and so is God."

Krystal spoke again, "Oh, really? I could have used help a long time ago!"

Tammi closed her eyes tightly, attempting to hold back the floodgate of emotions that raged within her. A tear made its way down her cheek despite her attempts to hold back. When she opened her eyes, she met Mackenzie's, also filled to the brim with tears, ready to overflow. *What was her secret?*

"Don't you all see?" Lauren pleaded. "You've never been alone. Think about it." She paused as if to let her words sink in. "God has gone to great lengths to bring the four of you together. Even though each of you is so different, he's used your pasts—your secrets, your pain—to draw you to one another and to him. But the devil has used your secrets too. To keep you angry, afraid, and alone. It's time to get it out in the open. It's time to be free!"

Tammi gasped, feeling like her air supply was being cut off. She quickly placed her hands on her throat. It was as though something was pinching her windpipe. Her breaths were becoming thinner and thinner. She kicked her feet, flipping up the sheet on her bed. She couldn't breathe!

Sadie reached out her hand, laying it beside Tammi's. Krystal, Mackenzie, and Lauren rushed to the bed. Tammi's face was turning purple.

"She's choking!" Krystal screamed.

A fatally injured Bellian had used its last bit of strength to wrap its enormous claws into Tammi's throat. It growled and gurgled, blood oozing from its mouth. "You'll never sing again!" The beast wheezed.

Theo stepped back, allowing Silas, already in motion, to plunge his sword into the massive demon's side, rendering the final death blow. Bellian released its grip, ragged wings flapping violently, twirling, causing a great funnel of wind that grew bigger and wider. Theo and Philo jabbed their swords into the cyclone. Sparks like lightening flashed while the twister grew smaller until it vanished altogether. The evil Lord Bellian was gone.

Tammi released her hands from her throat and laid her head back on her pillow. She let out a deep breath, "I want," she struggled to whisper, "what ... you ... have." She slowly leaned forward, reached out and grabbed hold of one of Lauren's hands.

"She's talking!" Mackenzie said to Krystal, whose mouth was agape.

Sadie began to giggle and cry at the same time. "See, I told you!"

Lauren breathed a labored sigh, squeezing Tammi's hand. "Are you all right?"

Tammi smiled. "Yes," her voice cracked. "Never better."

"This is unreal." Krystal shook her head back and forth, moving around Sadie's chair.

Mackenzie edged in closer, just behind Krystal. "What just happened?" Her voice trailed off, looking at Lauren for answers. All the girls were.

Lauren's face was beaming. "Girls, listen to me," she said, glancing at each set of wide eyes. "The Lord is here. He is working to draw each of you to him. And he wants to do even more than this." She smiled down at Tammi. "Like bind up your broken hearts. To bring freedom in the areas that have held you in darkness like prisoners. He also wants to comfort you where you mourn. He wants to wipe away all of your hurts and fears." She took Tammi's hand and gave it a squeeze, then turned her attention to all the girls again. "Look, we didn't get to choose our DNA, who we were born to or when we were born. We didn't even get to choose many of our life circumstances. But—" She leaned forward, her hands now on her hips. "We *do* get to choose what kind of people we're going to be. Girls, we can't save ourselves. We need God's son, Jesus, for that. The question is, will you choose to let him?"

"Let him?" Krystal asked, her brows furrowed together.

"I'm confused," Mackenzie said. "If he's God, why doesn't he just make us?"

"Yeah. I thought he was like all powerful." Krystal said, but not in her usual condescending tone.

"God gives all of us free will to choose him. He didn't make us robots. Sadie knows," Lauren said with a smile and nod in Sadie's direction.

Sadie bit her lip and nodded back to Lauren. "Yes. I chose him when I was a little girl. My real mama told me how to ask Jesus into my heart. But after the fire that killed her, I wanted to go back to the apartment to see if anything was left. I just wanted something to remember her by. But firefighters said there was nothing left. There was nothing left but ashes." Sadie voice quivered. She hunched over, cupping her hands over her face.

Lauren backed away from the bed and closer to the wheelchair. She kneeled and wrapped her arms around Sadie's tiny frame, stroking her golden curls.

After a few moments, Lauren released her, and Sadie began to speak again, her voice still trembling, "Then I lived with my meth-head aunt who couldn't take care of me, so I went into foster care. Some terrible things happened to me." Sadie stopped and wiped her nose with the back of her hand.

Lauren grabbed a tissue from the stand near Tammi's bed and handed it to her. Sadie blew her nose and took in a deep breath. "Okay, I can do this." She sniffed. "But for some reason, I always believed that God would get me to a good family that loved him and went to church. And he did!" Sadie's eyes now glistened with tears of joy. "But I think God wants to heal those bad things that happened to me in foster care—the *secrets*."

"It can't be that easy," Tammi rasped.

"The saving part is," Lauren said. "All you have to do is tell Jesus that you're done trying to fix things yourself. Ask him to be in the driver's seat of your life. The healing part takes time. But I promise you, if he can take the ash heap of my life and turn it into something beautiful, I know he can do it for each of you. That's what we are girls—*beauties*. Each one of us. Beauties from ashes."

Sadie wheeled herself a bit closer to Tammi's bed, reached out her hand, and placed it on Tammi's. "Well, I'm in. Are you?"

Tammi nodded her head and whispered, "I'm in." She placed her other hand on top of Sadie's.

Lauren leaned over the bed, extended her arm and placed her

hand on top of Tammi's. "I'm in." Then Lauren looked over her shoulder to Krystal and Mackenzie.

Krystal's jaw was clenched tight. She turned to Mackenzie, looking straight into her eyes, while reaching for her hand. Mackenzie sucked in her cheeks, staring back at Krystal, then grasped hold, squeezing tightly. Together, they dropped their clasped hands on Lauren's saying in unison, "I'm in."

Silas and Philo stood at the end of the bed, breathing heavily. Silas pushed back his long hair that was stuck to the sweat on his forehead. Philo wiped the blood from his sword then sheathed it at his waist. The two angels looked at one another and chuckled.

Silas bowed his head. "I can hear the heavenly choir. Should we join them with Theo and the others now, sir?"

Philo's eyes glowed like torches, gazing at Lauren and the girls. He turned to Silas and said, "Let's sing from here for a while."

The corners of Silas' lips rose upward. "Yes, sir!" he said, and began to sing.

After several minutes, Silas looked to his commander. "Well, I guess our assignment is complete."

Philo's jaw tightened, his mouth a straight line. He put his arm around his comrade's shoulder. "Yes, for now."

THE END

The Truth About the Supernatural

Angels, demons, the devil, and a spiritual dimension: Are they real?

Let me first say, *Beauties from Ashes* is a fictional series written to draw your attention to spiritual matters and your heart to God. We don't know if demons and angels look the way I describe them in the book. We also don't know if they operate in the same way.

But we do know this:

Angels, demons, and a spiritual dimension are real.

The Bible says not only are angels, demons, and Satan real, they are powerful beings created by God. They are not human and do not live on earth. And they're not aliens, either. They live in another dimension—the realm of the spiritual. I know this sounds a bit mystical, but hang in there. We are going to look at what the Bible shows us about these beings, where they live, and what they do.

You're probably familiar with this verse from Genesis 1:1. "In the beginning, God created the heavens and the earth."

"The heavens" is the Biblical name for the spiritual world that exists in parallel to the physical world (what we can see). God created a multi-dimensional universe.

Let's pause here for a moment.

Dɪᴅ ʏᴏᴜ ɴᴏᴛɪᴄᴇ ᴛʜᴀᴛ Gᴏᴅ ᴄʀᴇᴀᴛᴇᴅ ᴇᴠᴇʀʏᴛʜɪɴɢ? This means angels and demons too.

> The Son is the image of the invisible God, the firstborn over all creation. For in him all things were created: thingsin heaven and on earth, visible and invisible, whether thrones or powers or rulers or authorities; all things have been created through him and for him.
> (Colossians 1:14-16)

The Son mentioned here is Jesus. God created everything through his Son.

Wʜᴀᴛ ᴀʙᴏᴜᴛ Sᴀᴛᴀɴ?

Satan was once the angel named Lucifer, created by God. The Bible describes Satan as an exceedingly beautiful angel. He was likely the highest of all angels, the anointed cherub (Ezekiel 28:12-15; Isaiah 14:12-15).

With both the angels and humanity, God gave a choice—free will. You see, God did not want us to be robots. In pride, Lucifer chose to turn against God's authority (Isaiah 14:13) and became the head of a kingdom of evil spirits called demons—his "angels" (Matthew 25:41). Basically, Satan wanted to "kick God off his throne" and rule the universe. But instead, God kicked Satan out of heaven (Isaiah 14:15; Ezekiel 28:16-17), along with one-third of the angels (now demons) who chose to follow Satan (Revelation 12:3-4, 9).

Satan is not God's equal—not even close. However, Satan's power both in the heavenly realm and on earth is great and should not be underestimated. He makes the bad guys we've seen in movies look like weak little babies. He has many names and none of them are good. Here are a few: Satan means "the hater, accuser" (Revelation

12:10). He is called "the great dragon," devil, Beelzebub, which means "lord of the flies." He's also known as "the ruler of this world" (John 12:31, 32).

GOD IS IN CONTROL OF EVERYTHING.

Not only is God the creator of everything, he is all powerful (omnipotent), all knowing (omniscient). He is present in every time and space (omnipresent), and he is eternal—with no beginning or end. He has always been and will always be (1 John 3:20; Psalm 115:3; Matthew 19:26; Psalm 119:7-10).

God's home is called heaven (Acts 7:55; Isaiah 63:15). He sits on a throne in heaven (Matthew 23:22; Hebrews 4:16) surrounded by adoring angels who serve him (Revelation 7:11; Psalm 99:1).

Although God's home is heaven, he is active in our world because of his desire for a relationship with the people he created. In fact, he loves people so much that he sent his Son, Jesus, to live among us and even die for our sins (more about that later). Now if that isn't being involved, I don't know what is.

While Satan and his forces are formidable enemies, Jesus Christ crushed Satan's power, fulfilling the prophecy of Genesis 3:15. The cross of Christ won the victory (John 12:31). "The prince of this world now stands condemned." (John 16:11), and Jesus will one day destroy Satan's power completely (2 Peter 3:10).

WHAT ABOUT GOD'S ANGELS?

Angels will never become, nor were they ever, human—and neither will humans become angels when they die. Angels are spiritual beings with intelligence, great power, emotions, and a will. They also have names and hold ranks—as in the military (1 Thess. 4:16).

They were created to serve God. The Bible shows that angels have different ranks, jobs, and appearances (demons too).

What do angels look like? When they appear to humans, they look like people but are unlike any human we've ever seen. The Bible describes an experience with an angel as terrifying. An example from Matthew 28:3 says an angel's "appearance was like lightning."

What do angels do? A lot. They praise, worship, and serve God, of course (Hebrews 1:6; Psalm 103:20). But another one of their main jobs is to help humans. The Bible says they are "ministering spirits sent to serve those who will inherit salvation" (Hebrews 1:14). That's us. They also battle demons, carry messages, bring answers to prayers, are instruments of God's judgment and more (Daniel 10:13; Jude 1:9).

The point of angels battling demons is to thwart their plans. God has the final judgment (Matthew 25:41; Revelation 20:10).

WHAT ABOUT DEMONS?

Demons are spiritual beings and enemies of God. Like God's angels, they are intelligent, powerful, have a will, have names, and hold different ranks (Mark 5:9; Daniel 10:13; Ephesians 6:12)

What do demons look like? There is no way to know for certain as they are spiritual beings. However, we know the following: some demons may look like frogs (Revelation 16:13). Satan looked like a serpent in the Garden of Eden and is referred to as "the great dragon" (Revelation 12:9).

"Satan disguises himself as an angel of light." (2 Corinthians 11:14). Remember, prior to Satan's rebellion against God, he was a beautiful being. Deception always wears a mask. Satan and the demons attempt to appear as servants, guides, and "light" for people.

What do demons do? They are all about deception and destruction. Demons work for Satan and seek to deceive us, tempt us, lead us away from God, and even destroy us (2 Corinthians 4:4; John 10:10; 1 Peter 5:8). They also battle God's angels who protect us (Daniel 10:13; Ephesians 6:12). Let's be very clear about something: demons use our weaknesses, vulnerabilities, personality traits, and more to keep us from the freedom found in Jesus Christ. Demons are not the only reason we struggle with difficult issues, addictions, and illness (including bulimia and depression as in the story). We live in a sinful and broken world. Demons merely take advantage of our struggles.

WHAT ABOUT THE SPIRITUAL REALM?

The spiritual or supernatural realm is the *real* world. Earth is just a shadow or copy of that spiritual world (Hebrews 8:5). Even our bodies are only "tents" that hold our spirit (2 Corinthians 5:1). These bodies are wasting away. But our spirits are the eternal part of us designed for the spiritual realm.

The heavenly realms have a bright side and a dark side. "Heavenly realms" can refer to both angelic and demonic activity.

The bright side is full of amazing beings and places (John 14:2; Revelation 21-22). The dark side of the heavenly realms includes places such as the Lake of Burning Sulfur—Hell (Revelation 20:10).

IS THERE A REAL SPIRITUAL BATTLE TAKING PLACE LIKE WITH KRYSTAL, MACKENZIE, TAMMI, AND SADIE?

Yes, there is a real spiritual battle taking place at all times. The battle is quite personal for each person. But here is the good news: God has given people what they need to fight, and God always wins! However, we must fight this battle God's way and with God's weapons. More on that in the next section.

HOW DO WE FIGHT THE SPIRITUAL BATTLE?

STEP ONE: GOD'S WAY

Fighting the spiritual battle God's way means we must first give our hearts and lives to his son Jesus. All power and authority were given by God to his son Jesus (Matthew 28:18). We cannot fight the spiritual battle on our own, because Satan and his demons are too powerful. We must have Jesus.

God loves all people and doesn't want anyone to be separated from him (1 John 4:10; 2 Peter 3:9). But there is something that always separates people from God: sin. "All have sinned and fall short of God's glory" (Romans 3:23). Not just some people—all people.

Brace yourself for the best news you'll ever hear! God provided a way to get rid of your sin and be with him forever, and it's as easy as ABC!

HOW YOU CAN BECOME A CHRISTIAN

A▯ADMIT

Admit to God that you are a sinner (Romans 3:23; Romans 6:23). Repent, which means to turn away from your sin (Acts 3:19).

B▯BELIEVE

Believe that Jesus is God's Son and accept God's gift of forgiveness of sin (Romans 5:8; Acts 4:12; John 3:16; John 14:6).

C▯CHOOSE

Choose to follow Jesus as your Lord and Savior (Romans 10:9-10, 13).

Now, say a simple prayer like this:

> God, I know I have sinned, and that sin has separated me from you. I believe you sent your Son Jesus as the only way back to you. I believe Jesus died on the cross, then rose again, and is alive. Please forgive me. I ask Jesus to come into my life as my Lord and Savior. I will obey you and live for you the rest of my life.

STEP TWO: GOD'S WEAPONS

Not only do we have God and his angels to help us in the spiritual battles, we also have supernatural armor and weapons.

For we are not fighting against flesh-and-blood enemies, but against evil rulers and authorities of the unseen world, against mighty powers in this dark world, and against evil spirits in the heavenly places.

Therefore, put on every piece of **God's armor** so you will be able to resist the enemy in the time of evil. Then after the battle, you will still be standing firm. Stand your ground, putting on the **belt of truth** and the **body armor** of God's righteousness. For **shoes**, put on the peace that comes from the Good News so that you will be fully prepared. In addition to these, hold up the **shield of faith** to stop the fiery arrows of the devil. Put on salvation as your **helmet**, and take the **sword** of the Spirit, which is the word of God. **Pray** in the Spirit at all times and on every occasion. Stay alert and be persistent in your prayers for all believers everywhere.

(Ephesians 6:12-18 NLT; emphasis mine)

We use **God's mighty weapons**, not worldly weapons, to knock down the strongholds of human reasoning and to destroy false arguments. We destroy every proud obstacle that keeps people from knowing God. We capture their rebellious thoughts and teach them to obey Christ.

(2 Corinthians 10:4-5 NLT; emphasis mine)

Lastly, but certainly not least, God and his mighty angels fight for you and with you

"The Lord himself will fight for you. Just stay calm." (Exodus 14:14 NLT)

About the Author

BECKIE LINDSEY is an award-winning poet, author, freelancer, and blogger. She is the editor of Southern California Christian Voice, a division of One Christian Voice, a national news syndicating agency. She is a major coffeeholic and enjoys a good book with a cat on her lap. She also loves to hike and hang out with family and friends. Beckie and her husband, Scott, have three adult children, two adorable cats and live in California.

Read on for Chapter One from the second book in the *Beauties from Ashes Series, The Uninvited.*

THE UNINVITED
BEAUTIES FROM ASHES SERIES: BOOK TWO

Chapter 1

BRYCE followed Krystal at a distance down the hospital corridor. He dodged behind a group of doctors when she turned in his direction, then backed into an open doorway and stood flush against the wall, holding his breath.

"Hey, get outta here!" said an angry voice.

Bryce exited the room in a hurry. His shoes squeaked when he sidestepped a nurse, who let out a little whimper. Back in the hallway, he looked left then right, but no Krystal. Thinking she'd probably gone down the elevator, he pushed the button and tapped his foot as he waited. The door finally slid open and to his relief it was empty. He leaned against the wall and pictured Krystal's eyes when he told her about kissing Mackenzie. At first, they were honey-colored pools but quickly became dark slits just before he felt the impact of her fist slamming into his gut.

Now they both think I'm a jerk. He shrugged. *Well, let's face it, even I think I'm a jerk.*

Everything was a mess, and he didn't know how to fix it. But somehow, he had to. After knowing Krystal for most of his life, there was one thing he *did* know. When she was angry, it was best to give her time to cool off or he could expect another slug or worse, a verbal lashing.

So, stalk her. That's a great plan! He shook his head, slowly hissing out air. *What am I doing?*

Ding! The door opened, and a woman with a screaming baby pushed her stroller in. He walked out only to discover it was the wrong floor. He turned and the door was shut. The sounds of the baby screaming could still be heard but echoing at a distance. He threw his head back toward the ceiling then slapped the down arrow button and waited. The elevator wasn't coming. He glanced around seeing a door with a sign that said "stairs".

One flight of stairs and another door led him directly into the parking lot. He jogged until he reached the parking structure where he spotted Krystal's car in the front row. He paused, ducking behind a truck. Poking his head around the side, he caught sight of her car again as she was fumbling for her keys.

Then there was a scream.

———

KRYSTAL took one look at the blood and her knees gave way. She leaned against the car to maintain her balance. She felt like she was breathing through a straw.

Bryce raced toward her. "What happened?" He reached for her hand.

Her finger throbbed in tandem with her heartbeat, pounding loudly in her ears. "I slammed my stupid finger ..." She squinted and rocked back and forth, clasping her hands. "... in the door."

Bryce put his arm around her. "Let's go back in." He nudged her forward. "It's a good thing we're at the hospital."

Krystal wobbled. The ground appeared to be moving. Tiny droplets of sweat formed on her forehead, and waves nausea were taking over. *Oh, no! Don't barf!*

Bryce stopped walking. "We gotta get it looked at, K."

"I'm gonna be sick."

Bryce helped turn her around toward the car. "Okay, just lean back and breathe." He stood directly in front of her, bracing both hands onto the roof. She stood between him and the car, head down with her eyes closed.

"You just need some air," he said, blowing softly.

Feeling a bit of relief, Krystal glanced up, noticing the muscles in his biceps. He wasn't the same scrawny boy she'd called her best friend since grade school. She drew in the scent of his aftershave. Her attraction to him waned when she remembered what he'd told her less than an hour ago: *He kissed Mackenzie.*

"We need to get in there. Can you walk now?" He brought one arm down, and brushed her cheek with the back of his knuckles.

Krystal still felt weak in the knees but couldn't distinguish if it was from Bryce's touch or her throbbing finger. She shook her head.

"Let me see," Bryce said taking hold of her hand. She jerked it away, wobbling again. Bryce drew her up into his arms and began walking.

There was an initial instinct to protest. *No! How ridiculous is this? It's only a finger.* And she was still angry at him too. But instead, she gave in and laid her head against his shoulder while clutching her hand to her chest, blood sliding down her wrist. When they passed through the automatic double doors, a woman from the front desk scowled in their direction.

"She slammed her finger in the car door."

The elderly clerk huffed and nodded. "Uh-huh, and emergency is around the back, but I'll see if anyone is available."

"Okay, I can stand now," Krystal said, meeting with Bryce's green eyes.

He gently lowered her, keeping an arm around her waist. "Let's sit down."

She nodded and shuffled to a nearby seat when a nurse approached. To the right of the nurse stood Mackenzie, bony arms folded, looking from Krystal then to Bryce with one quizzical brow raised.

Although exhausted, Krystal couldn't sleep. *Why not give us an 'off' switch, God?* Realizing she'd just spoken to a God she never thought was real before today, her mind raced with all that had happened. Like jumbled pieces of a puzzle, she attempted to put everything together. The argument with her mom and brothers. Surprising them by going to church for the first time. Going to the hospital to visit Sadie in a wheelchair and Tammi, her head wrapped like a mummy. Her heated conversation with Mackenzie about Bryce trying to kiss Mackenzie. Bryce! What were they—still friends or more? And what about this whole God business?

Her finger throbbed, and her head hurt. She flung away the comforter and switched on the light beside her bed. Swinging her legs off the side, she grabbed her phone. 12:30 a.m.

Krystal put on her robe and fuzzy slippers, then scuffed through the dark to the kitchen. Moonlight cast oddly shaped shadows in every direction. A familiar chill rose up her back, the tiny hairs standing straight on her arms. She quickly slapped the switch on the wall as she entered the kitchen. The light made such a difference and yet, she still felt uneasy. Sensing she was being watched, her eyes darted to the window over the sink then to the vertical blinds that were still open enough for someone to see in through the patio door. She quivered.

Unseen by Krystal, several sets of yellow and orange cat-like eyes watched through both the kitchen window and patio door. The little misshapen creatures seethed and hissed, some flapping their raggedy wings, some slithering up the side of the window, and some using their claws to make scratching sounds.

Scre-e-etch! Krystal jumped. She managed to whisper, "Okay, if you're real God, please help me not be afraid."

"Krystal?"

She spun around, almost smacking into her brother, Kamron. "Oh!"

"What's going on, you freak."

Krystal gulped and pointed. "Something made a noise. A scratching noise on the patio door."

Kamron squinted, his thick dark brows scrunching together. He walked to the door, pushing back the blinds and peering out. He turned on the porch light, then opened the sliding door. Poking his head out like a turtle, swiveling from side to side, he shrugged and closed the door.

"Don't see anything unusual." He ran his fingers through his messy brown hair. "I'm hungry."

Krystal rolled her eyes. Kamron and his twin, Kasey, were always hungry. He pushed a chair up to the cabinet above the stove. Although teenagers, all three kids still had their places to hide junk food from their mom. Standing on the chair in his plaid boxers, he opened the small wooden door, pushing aside a cookbook and a weird-looking kitchen appliance, then retrieved a box of Ho Hos.

"Want one?" he said, while ripping the package, glancing down at her.

"What's that?" Krystal pointed up to something toward the back of the open cabinet. Kamron lifted his chin, then gently pulled out a glass bottle. He stared at the label without looking at Krystal. "Vodka," was all he said.

Krystal sucked in her lower lip. "Maybe it's really old. Maybe mom forgot about it."

Who was she kidding?